All rights reserved. No part of this book may be reproduced in any form by any electronic or mechanical means including photocopying, recording, or information storage and retrieval without permission in writing from the author.

Nothing As It Seems
Paperback Copyright © 2021 Lorhainne Ekelund
Editor: Talia Leduc

All rights reserved.

ISBN-13: 9781989698518

Give feedback on the book at:
lorhainneeckhart@hotmail.com

Twitter: @LEckhart
Facebook: AuthorLorhainneEckhart

Printed in the U.S.A

NOTHING AS IT SEEMS

A Billy Jo McCabe Mystery

LORHAINNE ECKHART

A New Crossover Series!

The Billy Jo McCabe Mystery

Nothing As It Seems
Hiding in Plain Sight
The Cold Case
The Trap
Above the Law

The social worker and the cop, an unlikely couple drawn together on a small, secluded Pacific Northwest island where nothing is as it seems. Protecting the innocent comes at a cost, and what seems to be a sleepy, quiet town is anything but.

The Social Worker

Billy Jo McCabe wants only to help children overcome their troubled lives, as she herself struggles to forget the childhood nightmare she survived. She took sociology and prelaw at the insistence of her adoptive father, Chase McCabe, and learned how to use power tools from her adoptive mother, Rose. She loves reading in the backs of bookstores before tucking the book back on the shelf and slipping out without paying. She has a fondness for peanut butter and dill pickle sandwiches, has a three-legged cat named Harley, hates running (because that was all she did as a kid), and secretly binges on brownies and red wine on the sofa in front of her TV every Friday night.

She's never been married and has dated only twice. She visits Chase and Rose when summoned and shows up dutifully for every holiday with her family, but she has no siblings to speak of, and she feels a growing resentment for the mother who abandoned her in foster care. Despite proudly maintaining the same prickly attitude that nearly landed her behind bars as a kid, she has yet to speak up to Chase, who interferes in her life too frequently, ready to fix every problem, whether she wants him to or not.

One thing no one knows about Billy Jo is that she moved to Roche Harbor because it's the only clue she has about the last known whereabouts of the woman who abandoned her.

The Cop

Mark Friessen, son of Jed and Diana Friessen, has landed accidently in the role of small-town detective, a position in which he's going nowhere. Nearly married once, and broken-hearted three times, he's sworn he'll stay single forever, and he keeps his tattoo of a former girlfriend as a reminder that only fools fall in love. He's tall, attractive, and stubborn, and he refuses to live in the shadow of his two older brothers, Chris and Danny.

As Roche Harbor's youngest detective, he sleeps with a gun under his pillow. He has a stray dog that won't leave, and he swears that the only two food groups that exist are meat and potatoes. His favorite drink is black coffee in the morning, sugared coffee in the afternoon, and a shot of whiskey in his coffee at night to keep him warm.

****Each book in this series is a complete book, with no cliff-hangers, and can be read as a standalone. However, these books may contain references to situations from earlier books in the series. As with any long book series that focuses on specific characters, their changing relationships, and how their lives continue to unfold, you may find it more enjoyable to read the series in order of publishing, as there will be developments and changes in the relationship dynamics of the core characters.*

"A compelling story that touches on powerful social issues"

(Bookbub Reviewer)

"The first book in a new crossover series that brings together members of the McCabe and Friessen families, and it is definitely an enthralling read."

Rebmay

"This is the beginning to a new series that promises to be just as explosive and compelling as the Friessen series."

Kathy

NOTHING AS IT SEEMS
A BILLY JO MCCABE MYSTERY, BOOK 1

From *NY Times* & *USA Today* bestselling author Lorhainne Eckhart comes the first book in the thrilling Billy Jo McCabe series, which unites two characters from The Friessens and The McCabe Brothers.

Billy-Jo McCabe never expected to become a social worker, considering the broken system nearly destroyed her. Shortly after she takes a job on a remote Pacific Northwest island, she gets a call about a missing girl.

Meanwhile Roche Harbor detective Mark Friessen is called in to investigate the disappearance, but instead of working with the newly appointed social worker, he ends up butting heads and clashing with her every step of the way. Billy-Jo becomes the rival he does his best to avoid, considering the only conversations they have involve her pointing out his shortcomings and arrogance.

But when Billy-Jo finds herself in over her head, she's

forced to team up with the man who has the uncanny ability to bring out the worst in her and together, they come up against close-mouthed locals, island secrets that hit too close to home, and the realization that their case about finding and helping a young girl has turned into something far more sinister.

Chapter 1

"Have you ever seen a more stunning place in all your life?" said the woman leaning beside Billy Jo against the ferry railing. She had a short blond mane, shapely curves, and long, long slender legs, wearing a red skirt and tank top that left little to the imagination.

Billy Jo knew the woman wasn't talking to her.

"Sure," came the reply from her other side, "if you love bad coffee, misbehaving tourists, weekend partiers, overpriced food, general mischief, and trash tossed everywhere on the beach every night and every morning."

What was it about his voice, deep and brooding? She took in the guy. He had on a worn jean jacket, blue jeans, and sunglasses, giving off that bad-boy vibe she knew girls loved.

"Well, that's a negative outlook of such a beautiful place," said the blonde. "Are you visiting or are you a local? Oh, let me guess! You live here."

Billy Jo wondered whether she should step back so

she wouldn't be in the middle of this pickup, knowing well that the blonde was working this tall, ruggedly attractive guy. Even she had shamelessly allowed herself to ogle him discreetly from behind her own shades. There was just something about the man who was leaning against the railing—pensive, quiet, brooding. He would likely be first in line to get off the ferry when it finally docked, and she'd be second off this rattling bucket of steel.

This time, the man actually glanced her way. She wondered whether he thought she was going to add something, but she refused to look up from her cell phone after seeing the latest text: *Check in with the chief of police as soon as you get there. He wants to meet you. Oh, and we got a call about a possible situation.*

She took in the grime on the steel deck of the ferry. Beside her were two hardtop suitcases, one large and one smaller, both thankfully on wheels. She could see from her peripheral that the man was watching her shamelessly from where he leaned.

Just then, the horn blasted to announce their approach, which had her jumping and the woman beside her shrieking. She swore under her breath, because what did that good-looking asshole do but laugh at both of them? She wondered if it was at her expense or the blonde's.

She glanced at some litter in the corner, which no one had bothered to clean up, and pulled up the handle of one suitcase. As the ferry jerked, she had to take a step to keep her balance.

"That was so loud," the woman said, actually leaning over to her as if they were the best of friends. "Don't they warn you?"

The hot guy was still laughing under his breath as if this were his daily source of entertainment. His hair was red, striking, short and messy. She knew the girl was flirting, whereas he seemed to be playing that not-interested game. He was tall, attractive, likely with the kind of alpha personality she was quite familiar with.

She wasn't impressed.

She needed to disembark, both from the swaying motion and the fact that apparently, there was a situation she had to check into. She didn't like situations, because they always came with the kinds of questions no one wanted to answer.

"It's a ferry," Billy Jo said. "They're loud and noisy."

And crowded, she thought, as the only way off and on the island. Now she was wondering at the wisdom of taking a job here.

She realized he was looking right at her from where he leaned, and she found herself under his scrutiny, dragging his gaze between her and the blonde. Maybe he was comparing them.

"Let me guess," he said. "You girls are here to do all the tourist stuff and look for a good time, or trouble, or something."

She realized he was including her in his evidently pretty low opinion, and she had to fight the urge to glance over to the blonde. She couldn't do that, though, as she was now pretending to look at her phone, which she held in one hand. Her bulky purse, which held everything else, was tucked over her shoulder. She pulled in a breath to set him straight.

"Oh, we're not together," said the blonde. Of course, she had jumped in. "Nora Cassberger is my name, and I'm on my own—totally, not that it wouldn't be fun hanging with you and everything…" She touched Billy Jo's shoulder, and her gaze went right there to her hand. Seriously?

Just dock the damn ferry, already! This was totally humiliating, and she had things to do, like find out what the hell this mysterious situation was.

The guy pulled down his sunglasses just a bit so she could see the most amazing, brilliant blue eyes. The guy seemed to ooze trouble. She wasn't sure what to make of his unsmiling expression or the way he didn't seem at all embarrassed to stare at her and then the blonde. *Right, Nora.*

Maybe this hadn't been such a great idea, standing at the front of the ferry, in front of the cars, so she could be one of the first off. But she was counting the seconds, and then she'd never have to see this guy again.

She forced herself to give everything to her cell phone and ignore him, because nothing good ever came with a guy who looked like that.

"I don't remember seeing you here before," he said. "You just another visitor, or do you have a reason to be here?"

Was he talking to her? The question seemed more like a demand.

Just then, her phone dinged with a sixth message from her dad, Chase McCabe, about her car, her cat, and the rest of her things, which he would be bringing over himself. She had insisted on moving away, starting a new life in a new place, looking for answers to questions she wasn't about to share with anyone.

She pulled in a breath to answer the jerk, this time powering off her phone and tucking it in her purse.

"You know, not that it's any of your business, but…" she started.

He was now looking over at the blonde as if he hadn't been talking to her.

Asshole!

For a moment, she considered stepping back, but the dock was right there, and she would soon be able to get off this damn ferry and out of this awkward situation.

He was leaning on one arm now, looking right at her, not the blonde. This had to be a joke. Her mud-brown hair was nothing special, and she had freckles over her nose. Her plain face was without makeup, and her capris and dark blue shirt were not only baggy but also comfortable. She wondered if she made a face.

She finally glanced over to Nora just as a gust of wind blew her skirt up, revealing black lace and killer thighs. Nora shrieked, and Billy Jo just shook her head, so glad she hadn't done anything stupid like wear a skirt.

Nora laughed then, and the way he stared—no, ogled, she knew he was just another guy who enjoyed the show. "I guess someone should have warned me about the wind," Nora said.

Billy Jo could feel her jaw slacken as she rolled her eyes. Seriously?

"I'm just here for a little getaway, is all," Nora continued. "Maybe you could recommend something fun, you know, touristy stuff, like great restaurants, night-clubs, anything like that. I mean, where is your favorite place to hang out?"

"Hey, Mark, smoke!" one of the ferry workers shouted to the bad boy beside her, gesturing to a cloud of black smoke wafting up just as the ferry docked.

She found herself looking to where he was pointing,

a smaller house on the hill, past the line of cars waiting to get on. She heard him swear under his breath. Just then, there was a *pop-pop-pop*, followed by screams and shrieks.

"Get the ramp down!" Mark yelled.

Pure instinct had her ducking and crouching behind her suitcase. She knew well the sound of a gunshot. Mark moved under the rope. Evidently, he was someone important, and she found herself really looking at him from where she was crouched. The metal gate was still closed, but the ramp was coming down. Mark hopped the metal fence in his cowboy boots and was on the ramp as soon as it was down far enough.

"Keep everyone here until it's clear!" he shouted, jogging up the ramp.

There was a loud boom, followed by another dark cloud of smoke and another *pop-pop-pop*. What the hell? This was supposed to be a safe, quiet island, not some crazy city.

She listened to the shrieks, people ducking and taking cover, though the ferry worker wasn't. Something about his demeanor told her this wasn't anything unusual.

"What do you think happened? Are we under attack?" Nora said, crouched right beside her, almost touching her. She realized the few passengers that had been standing behind her, waiting to walk off, were gone. Apparently, they'd taken cover, whereas she was right out in the open.

"I have no idea," she said.

Another ferry worker appeared, younger, tall, lanky, his pants two sizes too big, with not a care in the world. She could no longer see Mark running. Just who the hell was he? The ramp was now down, and people were in their cars. One of the ferry workers was talking on his radio as he stood in front of the metal gate, holding the latch, the only thing keeping it closed, waiting for… what? Why the hell weren't they concerned?

"Excuse me, what's going on?" Billy Jo called out from where she was still crouched, really questioning what the hell she was walking into on this island. "Is that gunfire, someone shooting?"

"Ah, just CJ Krantz," replied the ferry worker, "one of the old-time locals. Always something going on up there. Has a mess of guns he shoots off when the visitors here get too crazy for him, too noisy, bothering him. He says there are just too many of them here, so he shoots off a few pops in hopes of scaring people away. He's harmless, though."

Harmless… Was he kidding?

She heard a crackle over the worker's vest radio, and she slowly stood up. The smoke was fading, and there had been no more pops. She spotted who she thought was Mark putting out a fire with a hose, then heard a siren as a firetruck pulled up at the house.

The ferry worker lifted his hand and circled it. "All clear! You can unload," he called out to the other worker.

Billy Jo just stared in horror, because she knew well that guns and crazies weren't a good mix. "Whoa, just wait a second. You said this was a local shooting off guns? And is that a fire?" She gestured to the small old house, still seeing smoke from under the water. A few other people were up there now. Nora was holding her arm, and Billy Jo glanced back at her, taking in the spooked look.

The ferry worker just shrugged. "Mark took care of it. Likely a propane tank exploded on the barbecue at the back of the house. It's all under control."

"Wait, but that was gunfire—and who is Mark?" she asked.

The ferry worker pulled open the gate and gestured to her, and she knew to move. "Mark is a detective here on the island. He knows CJ and his shenanigans. He likely had the barbecue too close to the house. He's up there now, so the gun situation is handled. Don't worry, and welcome to Roche Harbor."

Something about the way he said it made her suspect he took some enjoyment in what had happened.

Great. So much for a sleepy, quiet place. She wondered what other surprises she'd be in for. She took a step, pulling on her suitcases, and the blonde fell in beside her.

"That was exciting! And that was a local cop? Wow, do you think he's single?" Nora said, still talking to her as if they were friends or something.

Billy Jo just stared at her. "I have no idea," she said.

But she did know that guys like that were exactly the kind of trouble she'd made a point of keeping off her radar.

————————————————————

Chapter 2

————————————————————

She closed up her empty suitcases on the small double bed of the furnished apartment she was renting. Having put away the last of her clothes in the chest of drawers, she took in the cute small bedroom. Its window had an ocean view of what she had already been told was a quiet part of the island.

She stared at her cell phone. The speaker was on, and she listened to the ringing: one, two, three… It went to voicemail again.

"Hello, this is Grant Webber. I'm either in a meeting or on the other line. Leave a message."

She wanted to scream as she reached for the phone. How many messages had she already left? "Hi, Grant. This is Billy Jo again, leaving yet another message. Listen, I'm at my new place and still waiting for a—" She heard a click.

"Hey, Billy Jo," Grant said. "So sorry about that. I was called into a meeting, so I only just got all your messages. Sorry to dump this on you before you had a chance to get settled."

Something about him had always set her on edge, the way he'd text or call her about a situation with a sense of urgency and then leave her hanging, like now.

"Well, you texted me, and it sounded urgent," she said. "You said there's a situation." She stared at the phone, squeezing it in frustration, glad he couldn't see her as she gestured.

He was talking to someone else in the background now as if she'd been forgotten—just something else about him that frustrated her. She could almost picture his messy tie over a plain dress shirt with brown stripes, his thick mustache, and his belly, which was always hanging over his belt.

"Right, right, here it is…"

She could hear papers rustling in the background and had to fight the urge to yell at her boss to hurry the fuck up.

"Ah, yes. There's a wilderness camp there on the island for troubled kids, a pilot project. It seems one of the girls there, Shay Williams, thirteen, in and out of juvie, has disappeared. No one has seen her since bed-check last night, etc.…"

Her frustration with him ramped up, because while he was reading a file, she had her boots on the ground, dealing with living, breathing kids who had feelings and cried and bled.

"Anyone call the police to report her missing?" she said.

More papers were rustling in the background, and now he was making that weird noise with his mouth that told her he was reading something—as if he hadn't just texted her about a problem. "They've been notified, the local yokels. It's a small island. There's a note here about marks on the girl. One of the camp counselors noticed, but hey, it's probably nothing. I mean, you know these kids. If they're not beating on each other, they're creating some other problem. She's got a history of running. Anyway, I've emailed her file to you. Check into it, but it's likely nothing. She probably went out for a hike and got lost, or she's in the wind, running again. We'll lock her back up. Juvie is likely the best place for her to stay until she ages out of our hands."

She wondered, as she listened to her boss talk, when he'd become such an asshole. "I'll check into it. I'll take a drive out there, and…"

Right, her car still wasn't there. Maybe, if it was close, she could walk.

"Oh, and don't forget to check in with the chief of police there," Grant said. "He's expecting you."

She wondered for a moment what took precedence, the missing kid or making nice with the police chief.

"Oh, and, Billy Jo, if she's running, turn it over to the police and let them handle it. I don't want a ton of resources wasted on this. We have a budget…"

"Yeah, I know. You can allot only a certain amount for one kid." She didn't try to hold back the sarcasm dripping from her tone.

"That's not what I meant. Of course she matters. I'm just saying, our resources are thin, so we have to pick and choose…"

This time she only nodded, rolling her eyes and keeping her mouth closed, knowing he was expecting her to agree. "Anything else?" she bit out as she strode out of her bedroom, breathing in the fresh pine of the wall paneling. Everything in this garage apartment was new.

She walked to the open front door, spotting Lesley Lancaster, her landlady, walking across the yard, plump, in green polyester slacks, with a basket, heading right for her stairs. She lifted a hand and waved, smiling, happy, with no idea how prickly Billy Jo could be.

"Nope," Grant said. "But, again, file your report as soon as you check it out so we can file this away. And remember the police chief. Mind your Ps and Qs." Then he hung up.

She squeezed her phone. Lesley, who owned this property, was now at the bottom of the stairs and climbing up.

"Hello, Billy Jo! Hope you don't mind me popping in like this, but I wanted to bring you some of my lemon blueberry muffins, a kind of welcome to the island."

Billy Jo was barefoot as she stood on the porch, waiting for Lesley, who she thought was in her mid-fifties. She held a small basket covered in a red checked napkin, and Billy Jo could smell something freshly baked. Her mouth watered.

"You made me muffins?" Billy Jo said. "Like, just baked in an oven from scratch?"

Lesley walked right into her apartment, and she followed her over to the small island, with its French press, two mugs, and pouch of coffee next to a tea sampler, another gift from her new landlords.

"It's the least I can do," Lesley said. "Consider it a housewarming gift. You have no idea how happy Lorne and I are to have a nice lady like you renting this suite from us. I know it's above the garage, but this is Lorne's baby. He took the better part of the year to build it. We briefly considered doing an Airbnb, but then, having strangers here every week for a few days sounded like a recipe for something to go very wrong. I told Lorne no, no, and no. So just know, having you here, we're so pleased. And a social worker, too! Are you getting settled okay?"

Billy Jo took in the thick warm-toned cushions on the log sofa and matching chair, which she was positive Lorne had made from trees from the property. The small dinette, with two wooden chairs, also looked brand new.

Lesley was likely going to be invading her space every day, she realized as she allowed her gaze to linger on the huge front window, which looked out on five acres of trees to the ocean. There was something about all of it… She couldn't help but feel her stress melt away.

But then, she still needed to deal with this situation at the camp.

"Yeah, just finished unpacking, and thanks again for picking me up at the ferry. That was really nice of you."

The woman just waved a hand at her. "The least I can do. I could see you were kind of rattled, having old CJ's shenanigans as your welcome to the island. But I have to tell you, other than that, he's harmless."

She needed to find a way over to the camp. "Right, just an old guy who has a lot of guns, loaded guns, which he shoots off at tourists, and blows up his barbecue. What's there to worry about?"

"Ah, the bullets are blanks, and he shoots them in the air," Lesley said. "He's been warned by the chief to knock it off, but every year at this time, when the visitors become crazy and impatient, we usually expect this kind of ruckus. He hopes to scare folks away, but they just keep coming. Oh, and I almost forgot! Since you probably don't have time to shop, I stocked up on groceries, just some essentials in the fridge and cupboards. And if you need anything, you just call or pop on over to the house anytime."

She wondered if the woman ever stopped talking. "Well, speaking of… My car is still not here, and I kind of have a work situation I have to handle. I wonder if I could borrow—"

Just then, there was a honk and the sound of a car, and Lesley turned. She could see her gray Corolla through the window.

"Oh, scratch that! There's my car," Billy Jo said. *And my dad and my cat.*

Billy Jo followed Lesley out onto her small deck, spotting the man behind the wheel, Chase McCabe, her father. She shoved her feet into her sandals as Lesley hurried down the steps ahead of her, lifting her hand in a big wave and heading over to the car.

Her dad stepped out. His blond hair was gleaming, as was the smile he gave everyone. He pulled off his shades and tucked them in his light blue shirtfront, and she couldn't believe he was actually wearing jeans.

"Hey, sweetheart," he called out, lifting his hand as she made her way to the bottom of the stairs and started walking his way.

"Well, I had no idea your dad was so handsome," Lesley said, tossing him a flirty look and an over-the-top smile.

"It's great to meet you, Lesley," was all her dad said.

"You let me know if you need anything, Billy Jo," Lesley said, then actually giggled and touched her arm before walking away.

All Billy Jo could do was nod, because this wasn't the

first time she'd seen this similar interest from a woman. She took in her dad's amused expression and the way he was looking at everything: the huge willow tree out front, the overgrown grass, which was brown and scorched, and the apartment built over the garage. The house Lesley and Lorne lived in was a two-story old-fashioned Victorian, white with green trim, with a welcoming front porch.

"You got here okay, I see," Chase said. "How is everything so far? Oh, and someone in the car is dying to see you." He pulled open the back door, and she heard a meow from the black cat kennel.

As she reached for the small cat carrier and lifted it out, her dad shot her an amused look. "So did he meow the entire way out here?"

"No, he gave me a two-hour reprieve while I was waiting for the ferry. I'll carry up the cat food, and you can show me around."

She knew this was just her dad's way of keeping tabs on her. "You know, you didn't have to drive my car out. I told you before that I'm a big girl who can stand on my own two feet and get myself here…"

"Your car was barely running," Chase said. "You would've broken down in the middle of nowhere if I hadn't made sure it was serviced. You should know the brakes had barely anything left on them, two of the rotors had to be replaced, and one of the headlights was burnt out."

She wanted to roll her eyes. Her dad was always shoving his nose into everything she did, as if he still needed to manage the misfit he'd saved so many years before. Sometimes she still felt like that terrified kid who'd been one step from life behind bars.

She could hear her dad behind her on the stairs as she walked inside her apartment, where she set the cat carrier down on the floor and opened it to scoop out her orange and white cat, Harley, who was missing his right front leg. As soon as she held him, he purred.

"Your mom said to remind you to take time off for Thanksgiving. We expect you home, no excuses," her dad said as he took in her place and the surrounding property. She didn't have a clue what he was thinking. With him, it could've been anything. "You can bring the cat too if you want. Don't forget to call your mom and let her know you're settled. You talk to your boss here yet?"

He was still looking around, but his blue eyes settled on her when she didn't answer right away. There was just something about her dad getting in her business; she wanted to remind him that she had two feet and could stand on them all by herself, and she knew he would hear her out, but she suspected her dad understood parts of her that she didn't share with anyone else.

"Yes," she said. "As a matter of fact, I just got off the phone with him, and I have a situation I have to check into. As I've been reminded twice, the police chief is apparently waiting to meet me. But I know I promised you we'd go for lunch when you got here, and I know how you are and how you want to check out this island and everyone you can before you have to leave. I'm sure you've already figured out some way to manage my life here…"

The way her dad looked at her, she knew he wasn't impressed.

"I'm not managing your life, Billy Jo," he said.

She put Harley down and opened the cupboard to

pull out a bowl, which she filled with water. Her dad had settled a big bag of cat food by the door, and he must have known what she was looking for, as he lifted it and put it on the table for her.

"Dad, you've been managing everything about my life since you met me. Wasn't it you who insisted I take sociology and prelaw in school? I'm positive you would've set up an office so I could work for you, and, for that matter, I'd still be living with you and Mom. You'd be deciding everything about my life, organizing me, telling me what to do…"

"Okay, stop, already," he said. "You know I did that only because I love you, and you really didn't have any viable options in mind for what you wanted to do. Yet here you are, working as an underpaid social worker…"

"You mean a much-needed social worker," she said, cutting him off. She wasn't about to be talked out of that choice, but with Chase McCabe, she found it difficult to stand her ground. "It's what I wanted. I didn't want to be a lawyer. That's you, and I think one lawyer in the family is enough."

She'd never seen her dad brood, but the way he let his gaze linger, she could see he was having a hard time with her living way out here. He shook his head and glanced at Harley, who was hopping on his three legs over to the sofa, so he reached down and lifted him onto the cushion. Even though Chase had complained constantly about Harley, his hair, and the fact that he was an absolute misfit, she knew he secretly liked him.

"Okay, I do really have to go," she said, "so how about I take you for lunch when I get back? I don't expect to be too long."

Her dad lifted his gaze, and a subtle smile touched his lips. "You want to buy me lunch?"

She shrugged. "Well, I'm sure it's the least I can do, since you had my car fixed and drove it out here, and now I'm running out on you."

"You know I would do anything for you," he said, turning so serious that she had to force herself to pull in a breath.

"I know you would. So what ferry are you on?"

Her dad walked over to the door, which was still open. "The one fifteen this afternoon. Your mom will pick me up on the other side," he said. As he looked around at her small, cozy place, she didn't miss the sadness. He had gone quiet, and she knew he was likely going to give her the third degree at some point that night, because that was just what he did.

His arms were crossed, and he seemed to consider something. Then he reached into his pocket for the car keys and held them up. She needed to get the hell out of here, because he didn't let anything drop.

"So, when you get back," he said, "I'd like you to explain to me again why you insisted on taking a job on this godforsaken island, getting half the pay you could, with lousy hours, when I had a perfectly good one lined up for you."

There was just something about her father. When he looked at her like that, she realized he knew her better than she was comfortable with.

"Why do you think this isn't the job I wanted?" she said. She wondered whether her nose grew, considering the only reason she'd searched out this job was because of the person she was looking for on the island.

"You seem to forget what I do, what I used to do.

When I got a call from the head of social services because you were asking about a job opening here, insisting on this place and only this place, I realized there was nothing coincidental about it. You hold your cards close to your chest, Billy Jo. You do this thing, though, when something is going on. I know well the way you evade and get secretive, the way you are now." He dropped the keys into her outstretched hand, and she had to remind herself to breathe .

There was one more thing about her dad: He was really good at tripping everyone up.

She forced herself not to look away, because this kind of interrogation was what her dad was exceptional at. "You ever think it could be because I wanted to live out on this island? This beautiful place, the quiet, the remoteness…"

Her dad laughed. "Now I know you're hiding something. You hate ferries, you hate the water, you hate the country. Are you going to tell me you've suddenly turned into an outdoorsy girl? As good as you are at hiding what you're thinking, what you're feeling, I'm better at finding out. I know you better than I think you know yourself."

Her phone dinged, and she pulled it out to see a text from her boss: *Need this wrapped up today!*

Chapter 3

The wilderness camp on the other side of the island was both remote and odd. The cabins were pretty rough, with no heat, and the bathrooms had only cold water. The kitchen building operated mainly with a wood stove. Although it was kind of cool to visit, something about the place didn't sit right with Mark Friessen, who took in the kids, the staff and counselors running the place. He had more questions than answers as he climbed out of his black Jeep TJ.

"Excuse me. You can't be up here," said a woman heading right for him down the grassy hill. She had dark hair pulled back and was wearing one of those wilderness T-shirts and blue jeans.

Mark pulled back his jean jacket to show his badge tucked into his waistband, as he could feel her getting ready to show him the road. "Mark Friessen," he said. "A call came in from someone at the camp about a missing girl."

Could he not make one trip off the island without

getting back in time for all hell to break loose? First CJ, now this.

"Oh, yes," the woman said. "Shay is gone. I put a call in to her social worker, as well. She was here last night, and we do bed checks, so everyone was accounted for, but this morning, her bed was empty, with no sign of her anywhere…"

He heard a car and turned to see a gray Corolla pulling in, stopping and starting as if the driver were confused about where to go. He couldn't quite make out who was behind the wheel, but he thought it was a woman.

"I'm sure you've already been told that for missing persons, there's a 48-hour—"

"She's thirteen, and she's in the care of the state," the woman said.

He wondered why the chief had forgotten to mention those details. He reached for his phone to check the text again. It was the chief's day off, and unless a body washed up or something pretty serious went down, he didn't cancel his day off.

Girl missing at wilderness camp. Check it out!

The counselor walked around him just as he heard a car door, and he turned to see a young woman stepping out from the Corolla, parked behind his Jeep. She had shoulder-length brown hair and wore blue capris and a matching blouse, baggy, like the outfits his mom would wear. She lifted her sunglasses to the top of her head. Something about her seemed familiar, maybe from a previous encounter.

Trouble with the locals? A lost tourist?

"Hi," she called out. "I'm the county social worker,

Billy Jo McCabe." She reached into her purse and pulled out her wallet and ID.

The camp staffer walked right up to the social worker to examine her ID, then nodded.

What was her name…Billy Jo? She looked right at him, and something about her expression and the way she looked at him told him she was pissed. Where did he know her from? He took a step and then another toward her.

"Jeanette Holmes," the staffer said. "I'm one of the counselors here. I was just talking to the detective when you pulled in." She pointed to him over her shoulder with her thumb.

Mark shoved his phone back in his pocket. It looked like all the kids out on the hill were wearing the same T-shirt, but some also wore hats. They were following one another in anything but an orderly line to one of the buildings.

"Detective Mark Friessen," he said again as he joined the women. "Again, I have to say this: Maybe you're jumping the gun by sounding the alarm about her being missing. Thirteen, you said? She likely took off for a hike, a walk, and maybe got lost. It's not even noon. She's a kid. That's what they do."

"Excuse me," Billy Jo snapped. "If you don't mind, it sounds to me as if you have your mind already made up about the girl."

He felt the slap.

She turned back to Jeanette, who didn't seem to know where to look, and said, "Her name is Shay, is that right?"

It had been a long time since he'd felt a woman's

dismissal, but he was damn sure that was exactly what he was on the receiving end of now.

"That's right," Jeanette said, "Shay Williams. But it's more than that. I knew something was wrong. You just get a feeling when you work with these kids. I don't know her well or her home life, but she had some concerning marks on her. Most of the kids who come here have a story. Every single one of them comes dragging a ton of baggage."

"What kind of marks, exactly?" Billy Jo said. "I had only a brief chance to look at her file, and from the conversation I had with my boss, it doesn't sound as if we have too much information. I take it the call came from you?"

What was it about this woman? She wasn't looking at him, but he was trying to figure out where he knew her from. Was it the cafe in town, or had they met on another case? No, he remembered every case he'd worked since landing on the island eight months earlier.

"Excuse me," he said. "I know you from somewhere. Where, exactly, have we met? Because I'm pretty good with faces. Was it a case, a warning I gave you…?"

Her expression darkened. He really did have a way with women, but then, any time he considered getting close to a woman, he ended up burned. All the women he seemed to attract were cold hearted and difficult.

He realized Billy Jo was saying nothing, dragging her gaze so slowly from Jeanette over to him. Her eyes were brown, and her expression was scathing. What was the big deal? Maybe something had happened between them. He seriously hoped she hadn't been one of the women he'd picked up after a few drinks only to conveniently lose her number after.

He gestured toward her, because now he was in it. "I kind of like to know who I'm dealing with. You're a social worker here? But we've met—"

"You're kidding, right?" She cut him off. "A kid is missing, and you're more concerned about where we met?" She made a rude noise, and he found himself looking over at the camp counselor, feeling he was about to be dismissed again. "So, Jeanette, can you tell me about these marks on Shay and where they were?"

"No, just hang on a second, here," Mark said. "I'm the police, so I'll ask the questions."

There was just something about this woman. He suddenly felt as if he were about to be neutered. There was no way in hell he was about to fall under the foot of a woman again. Maybe he hadn't picked her up, after all. Maybe she was gay or just didn't like men, period.

She lifted her brow, about to challenge him. He'd known enough strong women to know when one was trying to tell him what to do.

"Jeanette, is it?" he said, turning to the counselor. "How about you tell me everything about this camp, this girl, all the staff here, and who last saw her? And, while we're at it, tell me about these marks you're concerned about. Who are her parents? Have they been contacted? And why are you so convinced something has happened?"

He spotted another man walking their way. He was about his age, he thought, with brown hair, wearing the same T-shirt, which had to be the camp uniform. He lifted his hand to them and said, "Hello, there. Can I help you folks? This is a closed camp, and visiting day isn't until Wednesday."

Jeanette crossed her arms. Billy Jo was staring at

Mark in a way that told him she was about to ignore anything he said.

"Todd, I told you I was calling the police," Jeanette said. "Her social worker——"

"And I told you that you were jumping the gun in sounding the alarm," Todd said. "You're going to jam Shay up. It's likely she went off alone. The kid has had too many tough breaks, so give her a good one here."

Okay, he kind of liked this guy, sort of.

Todd walked over to him. "I'm so sorry about this. Todd Spencer, head councilor. I'm responsible for everyone here." He actually held his hand out to Mark, who shook it but didn't miss Billy Jo's reaction, the way she rolled her eyes.

"Excuse me. Todd, is it?" She stepped over to them, and he took in how short she was, kind of like his sister-in-law, Evie, about five foot two, give or take, but she gave off a powerful vibe that she wasn't about to take anything lying down. "Let me cut into this boys' club and point out to you that Shay is a minor. I'm a social worker and have been sent in by the state, so let me be very clear that you have a responsibility to notify us immediately of any issues. If you're running things here, how about I start with you? Tell me about these marks on Shay and how long she's had them. I want to see her things and her cabin, then talk to everyone here."

Mark just stared down at her, feeling the challenge. The two counselors were leaning toward answering to her, this woman who still hadn't told him where they'd met. He wondered, in this mess, why that bothered him more than anything.

"Can I have a word with you?" he said, leaning in. This spitfire wasn't smiling and wasn't taking her cue from him. Maybe he needed to set her straight on how it worked here. "Now, over here?" He gestured with this thumb. "Excuse us for a minute, would you?"

The counselors stepped away, whereas Billy Jo crossed her arms and flicked her gaze up to him, pissed off, angry. He wasn't going to look too closely into that.

"Mark, is it?" she said. When he touched her arm to move her closer to his Jeep, she stared at his hand until he pulled it away.

"Sorry, my mistake." He lifted his hands. "I just want to have a word with you on how things work here. You're not in charge. If the girl's missing, this is a police investigation. You're, what, a social worker?"

Her eyes widened, maybe because of how he'd said it. But then, he had only two ways of talking to women, and right now he could feel her wanting to fight instead of sitting back and letting him do his job.

She raised a brow. "Mark Friessen, is it?"

The way she said it, the way he felt her lean in, he knew he wasn't going to like what she had to say. He angled his head and gave it a shake. Two could play this game.

"That's Detective Friessen to you," he said.

She laughed and shook her head. "Okay. You know what? Been there, done that. Let's be clear here. There's a missing girl in the system who could be hurt, for all we know, yet you're trying to get into a pissing contest about who has more authority. The only thing that should matter is this girl—who is thirteen, by the way, and likely hasn't had anyone give a shit about her, ever. So, if you don't mind, could you put away this disdain of yours and get over yourself already? The only thing I'm interested in is finding this girl and making sure she's okay, and then, if someone has hurt her, I need to make sure it doesn't happen again. Do we understand each other?"

As she stepped back, he realized where he knew her from. "You're the chick from the ferry," he said.

All she did was stare at him, then shook her head. "Right, and you're the asshole who thinks he's God's gift to women. Now, if you don't mind, I'd rather get back to more important things than you." She dragged her gaze down, and he could feel the slight, the jab.

"Actually, I do mind," he said. "You may be a social worker, but that's all you are. I'm the police and am in charge here, not you." He took a step past her, seeing the shock on her face as he shut her down. "Come over here, both of you," he called out, gesturing to the counselors. "I want you to run me through what the hell is going on here, and no one leaves anything out."

Chapter 4

Billy Jo had slapped her steering wheel a half dozen times as she called that arrogant cop every combination of four-letter words she could think of. She'd wanted to talk to everyone else at the camp, but what had Detective Mark Friessen said but no?

No!

Like, what the hell was that? After what had seemed like some over-the-top male bonding with Todd, the counselor, she had half-expected the detective to invite him out to the local pub for a beer or whatever it was guys did together!

Both men had been under the impression that she and Jeanette were overreacting, even though she knew they had to have heard all of her suspicions and the urgency. That was likely why she was imagining running the jerk detective over now as she geared down.

The engine revved way too loud. She hadn't realized how fast she was driving as her car hit a rut in the driveway going up to her place. The car went sideways, and she heard a clunk that didn't sound good. She jammed on the brakes, skidding across gravel and dirt.

She came to a stop at the bottom of her stairs, probably a little too close, and pulled up the emergency brake, then saw three sets of eyes staring at her from Lesley and Lorne's front porch.

"Oops, sorry," she said, more to herself than anything, as she turned off the engine and then opened her door.

Her dad stepped off the front porch. They'd all seen her pull in, crazed and out of control.

"Everything okay?" Lesley called out.

She gave her door a shove closed and didn't miss her dad's expression as he strode across the yard with purpose. Of course, he knew something was up.

"Sorry, yes," Billy Jo replied, really feeling like an idiot. "Didn't realize I was driving so fast. Sorry!"

The closer her dad got, the less impressed he seemed. She looked up to her front porch and spotted the door open, Harley looking down on her as if to agree with everyone.

"What's wrong?" was all Chase said.

Billy Jo pulled in a breath, ready to say it was nothing.

When he stopped right in front of her, he didn't have his sunglasses on, and she didn't miss the seriousness in his blue eyes. "Don't you dare say it's nothing, because I know you, and I know when something is bothering you or throwing you off your game. Now I know why your car was such a mess. If you're upset, don't take it out on your car. Don't take it behind the wheel, period." He pulled his arms across his chest. "I don't like leaving when you're like this. I can see that something has upset you. It didn't go well?"

She shut her eyes, but that was a mistake, because red hair and blue eyes were all she saw, along with the disdain and arrogance the detective had for her. The feeling was absolutely, one hundred percent mutual.

"No, it didn't. There was this guy…" She let her head fall back, because he wasn't just a guy. He was going to be a very real problem that would get in the way of her doing her job.

Her dad was still looking at her. "Are you telling me some guy here is giving you a hard time?" he said. There it was, that overprotectiveness that had always existed.

"Detective Mark Friessen," she said. "He's such a jerk. I went out to the wilderness camp because there's a missing girl, yet this detective basically shut down any search for her. You know, he actually believed I was overreacting. I'm not kidding. The head counselor over there, also a male, basically came out and said as much. Me! I do not overreact." She made herself pull in a breath. Her dad's sharp gaze was enough of a warning about how loud she was being.

"When you left, you didn't say what this was about or who. A missing girl, huh? How old? Here on the island?"

She wanted to groan. She couldn't be talking about this, but this was her dad. When she got upset, she went on a spiral, going into a rant, her mouth running like it was now. She shut her eyes for a second and touched her hand to her forehead.

Her dad was watching her, maybe trying to figure out how to fix this for her.

"Yeah, just a kid," Billy Jo said. "But it's more about the fact that one of the counselors, Jeanette, sounded the alarm and put a call in to the police. She said the missing girl had marks on her, that she refused to wear the T-shirt everyone in the camp does. Once, when Jeanette accidentally walked in on her when she was stepping out of the shower, she saw bruising on her arms that appeared old, as if someone had grabbed her too hard, and on her back and the backs of her legs, as if she'd been kicked.

"Even after hearing that, the detective wasn't all over this! He just stood there while the two counselors argued back and forth. The male counselor was saying they have no way of knowing whether someone hurt Shay or she did it to herself. Apparently, she has a history, and until they can get her in a chair and question her, no one can say for sure what happened and when."

She was pacing, and she lifted her hands and gestured to her dad. "Okay, I get it that none of us know for sure, and he could be right that it was one of the kids at the camp. But still, that damn arrogant detective said he'd make some calls. Then he basically ordered me to leave. There was a point there that—"

"You wanted to argue, defy authority, do what you wanted to do, to hell with anyone?" her dad cut in. He had said it so calmly, but she didn't miss the punch in his words. He really did have a way of seeing her in the most unflattering angle.

"You make me sound impossible, difficult."

There it was, the subtle tug of a smile at her dad's lips. "You don't make things easy at times, honey."

Maybe it was the way she frowned that had her dad

putting his hand on her shoulder and really looking at her as if he needed to make a point.

"You listen to me," he said. "It doesn't mean your mom and I love you any less. We love you with all these quirks of your personality. Some of these traits will make you a damn good social worker, because if you take that passion and that fight and use it for the kids you're trying to help, you'll move mountains. But at the same time, I have to caution you, you can also burn out…"

"From caring too much," she said. She wasn't sure how to take it.

Her dad rested his hand on her shoulder again, maybe to settle her. "Let me finish, Billy Jo. You butt heads with authority—at times with anyone. I know it. But you're in a field where you're going to be working with a lot of authorities, and you're not going to agree with them in some of the things they decide. If you go at some of them like this, you could end up hurting the kids you say you're trying to help, because doors will close, and those in power, with the authority to make a difference, will turn their backs on you and won't tolerate this kind of pit-bull attack."

She said nothing.

Her dad pulled in a heavy breath as he stepped back, then glanced up at her place. "Look, I have to leave soon for the ferry…or I can call your mom and tell her I'm staying."

"Dad, no. Go. I'm a big girl. You don't have to stay and fix this. I'm just…"

Her dad pressed his hand to her shoulder and gestured to the car. "Go up and put the cat in. Then you can buy me that lunch you promised, but it sounds like you may be off to a rocky start here on the island, butting heads with someone who can make things easier or harder."

She knew he was talking about the detective. She was about to dig in, to argue, when he gestured again, ready to tell her what to do.

"Billy Jo, you know this already, but in case I need to spell it out to you, sometimes being an adult and doing the right thing means you need to swallow your pride so you can make a difference to a kid who needs your help. If you want to find this girl, it sounds like you need the help of this detective. Mark Friessen, you said?"

The way her dad said his name, she had a feeling there was something more there, but he only shook his head.

"You want me to suck up to him, don't you?" she said. She could feel the growl inside of her, wanting to claw Mark's eyes out instead.

"No, I want you to be a big girl and find a way to form a truce, to get along with this detective to find this girl. Sometimes you have to work with people you don't like, so my advice to you is to dig deep and find something to like in him. Everyone has something. If that proves too much, tell yourself that if you don't, a girl who could be in trouble is the one who's going to pay the price for your pride."

Now, how did he do that? The words he used were like an icy splash of water.

But why did she have to be the bigger person here?

The problem was that she already knew the answer.

———————————————

Chapter 5

———————————————

"**M**ark, how many times have I told you? If you finish the coffee, put another pot on."

Mark was behind his desk in the police station, filling out another report about the missing girl and the fact that no one at the wilderness camp seemed to know anything. The problem with that was that someone always knew something.

The way the social worker had pulled out of there without another word to him, he knew that as long as this girl's case remained open, she would likely continue to be a thorn in his side.

"Didn't you hear me?" said Gail Shepard, the chief's wife. "I'm not your mother, you know. Taking the last of the coffee and shoving the pot back on the burner is not only a fire hazard but also makes it damn impossible to clean all the burnt-on crud."

He lifted his gaze to her. She wore a brown cardigan over the Roche Harbor Police Department T-shirt and a pair of blue jeans. He supposed her light shoulder-length hair had once been blond, and her hazel eyes often found humor. She didn't pack a gun, ever, because she only ran the office and showed up when the chief wasn't in. Maybe that was why they were still together after thirty years.

He realized she was expecting him to answer. "I see we're out of sugar. Had to take my coffee black." He leaned back in his chair.

She shook her head as she kept walking. "You always take your coffee black, Mark."

"I take my morning coffee black," he said. "Afternoon coffee calls for sugar."

And for coffee at night, he added a splash of whiskey, though she hadn't figured that out yet.

He lifted the coffee and took a swallow of the bitter brew, then glanced to the door of the office as it opened, and who walked in but the very thorn in his side, that damn social worker, Billy Jo?

He really didn't feel like going another two rounds with this lady. Whatever she was saying to Gail, she was smiling—which he hadn't thought was possible.

"Mark, visitor," Gail called out to him, gesturing.

He didn't move from where he reclined in his old office chair. Instead, he put his mug down and closed up the case file on his desk just as Billy Jo approached. The smile disappeared the closer she got.

He made no move to stand up even though he could almost hear his dad in his ear. *Show some respect!* She was still a lady, and he knew his dad would likely have given his ear a tug. Maybe that was why he had to fight the urge to roll his shoulders. He was the one in charge here. He was the cop.

He could feel the argument coming as she dragged her gaze over his desk, pulled her arms across her chest, and stopped in front of him. But she didn't say anything for a minute.

He figured two could play this game. He thought he should feel awkward about staring at her so blatantly, but he didn't. He really could be an asshole when he wanted to be.

"Yes...?" He gestured quite rudely, then rested his hands back over his belt buckle.

"I understand the chief isn't in," she said. So that was who she was there to see. He wanted to laugh, because she wouldn't be the first woman to want to go over his head.

"It's his day off," he said. He realized he could have done the polite thing and asked her to sit, or maybe he could've stood, but leaning back and ogling her was more his style right now. There was just something about her that brought out the fight in him.

She nodded and then lifted her hands. "Fine, so when will he be in?"

He said nothing for a second, shamelessly allowing his gaze to drag down over her and back up. He wondered how long she'd stand there and just take it.

She didn't move, and she didn't seem embarrassed in the least. He was positive something flashed in her eyes, which simmered with the kind of anger that should've been a warning to him. He pulled in a breath, because it seemed she wasn't someone to fill the silence, though he thought that was something women were known for.

"You can try him on Monday," he said. He could have said anything else, and he didn't miss the way Gail was now watching him from behind her desk at the other end of the bullpen. Evidently, she had figured out there was an issue.

"Honey, he's off on weekends," she said. "If it's urgent, I can get him a message, but otherwise, Mark here will look after you. Right, Mark?"

He didn't miss the motherly warning.

"What can I do for you, Billy Jo?" he said, gesturing again, though he had no intention of getting up.

"Well, I would like to go back out to the camp and have another look around. I've made some calls, and apparently there are two girls Shay bunks with. I'd like to have a word with them. Also, I'm not really sure what the procedure is here for starting a search party."

He said nothing, just stared at her. He could see there was way more she wanted to say. Evidently, she'd done her own digging after he pulled the two counselors aside and had a word with them. He was still convinced the girl would turn up. It was an island! It wasn't as if she could just walk off. He'd planned on making a few more calls to her foster parents, anyone who actually knew her.

"Look, I don't like you," Billy Jo said. "I'm just going to say it. I think you're arrogant, and you could be a good cop, but I think you believe you're better than anyone else. You have a chip on your shoulder, or maybe you spend so much time looking in the mirror that it keeps you from figuring out that maybe, just maybe, if you let your pride go, you might actually get some work done here."

His feet hit the floor, and he stood up until he towered over her. It wasn't lost on him that she never stepped back as he moved into her space. In fact, all she did was look up. She didn't flinch, and there wasn't an ounce of wariness showing.

"You come in here and try to bust my balls…" he started.

All she did was angle her head. "I came in here because there's a girl out there, in trouble, and apparently, without the police stepping in, no one is going to look for her. Since you're it, fine, I'll be the bigger person and put aside my feelings. Now, again, a search party. I would like to get one started. She's probably lost and alone and scared. Then there's the question of the marks on her."

He pulled in a breath and pulled his hand down his face. "Look, I'm as concerned as you are, but we're not calling in search and rescue for a lost girl on the island right now. How we go about things here is that we put a notice in our community newsletter to check if anyone has seen the girl. This isn't the city. This is an island, and the only way off is the ferry, so someone has to have seen her. We also need a photo of her to put up."

Billy Jo reached into her purse and pulled out a laptop, then set it on his desk and opened it up. "I have her photo here. It's in her file." She turned the laptop to him, and he took in the dark complexion, the dark hair in a messy braid, and the dark eyes that didn't smile. It really did look like a mugshot. He had to remind himself he was the one in charge.

"Email it to me here." He pulled out a card with his name, phone number, and email and tossed it on the desk, and Billy Jo picked it up. He walked around her toward Gail, who was watching him make his way over. "Gail, can you put the girl's photo up on the electronic community notice? Let folks know to call the office and tell us if they've seen her."

The chief's wife lifted a brow. He thought more was coming as she leaned over in her chair to look around him at Billy Jo. "Sure," she said. "Anything there you want to tell me about?"

All he could do was shake his head. Something about the social worker brought out everything uncivil in him. "Nope. Oh, and she wants to have a word with the chief about me, evidently..."

Gail made a face. "Really? I thought it was the chief who asked her to come in." She glanced up with that look of hers that told him she knew way more than he did. "Because, after all, Mark, a new social worker on the island would be something the chief would want to know about. If you'd read the weekly newsletter I did up, you'd know we were expecting Billy Jo McCabe, and her first order of business was to meet the chief."

Why did it feel as if he'd just been reprimanded again?

"Just get the photo up," he said a little too sharply.

He turned back to see Billy Jo standing behind him, her purse over her shoulder and her laptop tucked back inside. Something about having his foot jammed in his mouth didn't sit right with him.

"So who, again, is it you want to talk to?" he said.

Billy Jo didn't smile as she pulled her arms across her chest. "The girls she bunks with. According to her foster parents, who shipped her off to this camp, she didn't have a mark on her when she left. So if something happened at the camp and there was an altercation with one of the other kids, maybe, just maybe, one of them knows where she is."

He made himself pull in a breath, and he looked over to Gayle, whose expression said everything. Why in the hell hadn't his first call been to the foster parents? Maybe because he didn't have the same information Billy Jo did.

"Fine," he said. "But before we go, I know you know something, and I want you to tell me what it is. Tell me what's in her file, because the sooner we find her, the sooner we can be out of each other's hair."

It was her expression that bothered him, the way she suddenly smiled so brightly. "That's fantastic. Let me pull out my file, and maybe we can have this wrapped up before the sun sets."

He heard a soft laugh from Gail, then gestured toward her. "Well, what are you waiting for? Get to it, already," he said—but he immediately knew he was going to hear from the chief for snapping that way, so he forced himself to take a step over to her and lowered his voice as he said, "Please, Gail, and thank you."

Chapter 6

S wallowing her pride was an understatement. Billy Jo had to remind herself of her dad's parting words before she'd dropped him off at the ferry after a quick bite. He'd basically done what he always had, figuring it was his responsibility to make sure she had her head screwed on straight.

She wondered whether he had any idea of the dark thoughts that often plagued her, the growing hate for a woman who had abandoned her.

Now, she found herself in the passenger side of an old black Jeep with takeout cups and packaging at her feet.

"You can just give all that a toss into the back," Mark said, and it took her a second to realize he was referring to the garbage. He wanted her to clean up after him as he drove along, bouncing over the ruts in the road. She knew the sigh came out sounding annoyed, but then, it was second nature when dealing with someone like this.

"You know I could've driven us, and then I wouldn't

be basically cleaning out your car for you," she said. "I mean, do you live in here? Seriously, this is like a garbage can." She picked up a plastic lid and spotted a bit of mold on the edge as she dumped it on the floor behind his seat, then wiped her hand on her capris. She reached for the three empty takeout coffee cups also on the floor.

"Do you ever not complain?" he said.

Arrogant and an asshole. Right, just breathe.

"So you're not going to answer?"

She pulled in another breath, then let out a cough from the dust. She reached for the handle of the window and rolled it down. Just the way he was talking, she could feel him poking at her, and she turned to see how comfortable he was. A man in his wheels, in charge. She realized now that he wasn't the kind of guy who could be convinced of anything easily.

"I don't complain," she said, "but I have a low idiot tolerance, and—"

He barked out a laugh, cutting her off.

"And might I point out that I'm the one who's putting her feelings aside to look for the missing girl, Shay?" she continued. "If finding her means I need to work with you and mind my Ps and Qs, then fine, so be it. I'll be the bigger person here. The sooner we can get to the wilderness camp, talk to the kids she bunked with, and get some answers…"

"I'm still waiting for you to fill me in on her file, who she is, everything," he said. "All you've done is complain. Might I also point out that this girl is in the system? She was at a camp for kids who know only one thing: trouble—attracting it, being in it, and getting up to it. So this kind of thing isn't that unusual."

The way he said it, she couldn't pull her gaze from him. She couldn't remember the last time someone had managed to get under her skin the way this jerk did. "I can't believe you just said that about her. Did you seriously just imply that her being a foster kid is the reason this has happened? Let me guess: You think she's not really of any importance because she doesn't come from the kind of family that matters." Her jaw ached as she bit out the words.

He slammed on the brakes so hard that the Jeep skidded, and if she hadn't been wearing her seatbelt, she'd have gone through the windshield.

"Hey!" she yelled. She'd have to be a fool to miss the fact that she wasn't winning him over. In fact, from his expression alone, she suspected he might very well dump her on the side of the road.

He wiggled the stick and put it in neutral, revving the engine. "Don't start down that road, and don't call me racist or uncaring. Let me be very clear, Billy Jo McCabe: I'm done with this attitude of yours, the way you keep arguing, coming at me and just being a pain in the ass. It doesn't matter whether she's from a rich family or poorer than dirt. A kid is a kid, and I'd look for either the same way. But I'm not going to be able to find squat if we're not being real, and being real means facing the facts and knowing exactly what I'm dealing with. Let me point out, by the way, that you've still shared squat about her. She's a foster kid, in trouble, in the system. If she has a history of running, I need to know, because that'll give me a clue where to start. Where does she run to? Does she have a person to call? Does she have a history of stealing, running, robbing gas stations…?"

"I pulled a gun at a gas station when I was her age."

The minute she said it, she wanted to take it back. She let out a breath and looked away, reaching into her bag on her lap. He said nothing, and she could hear the engine running. She pulled out her phone to open the file sent to her email, knowing he was still staring at her. She couldn't believe she'd said it, because she didn't tell anyone about her past, how she'd met her mom and dad, how that one moment had defined her whole life.

"Shay Williams was born in Tallahassee," she said. "Her mother is dead, shot in an altercation with the police. Her father is unknown, and there's no other family. She's been in the system since she was three. Doesn't say how she came to be out here, but she's just recently been in a juvenile facility in Leavenworth since an incident with her last foster family. Says here she has trust issues, anger issues, and is a runner. She's lived in six different homes. Oh, this is interesting. She has a twin sister, Shauna, but it doesn't say anything about where she is."

It took her a second to realize they were moving again.

"You said an incident with her foster family," Mark said. "Does it say in there what happened?"

She thumbed through the text, which seemed so incomplete. "Pulled a knife on a foster brother. The parents couldn't manage her and feared what she'd do."

"So she's dangerous," Mark cut in.

She lifted her gaze. He was turning into the camp. "Doesn't mean that, Detective. It means only that she pulled a knife. She could've had a reason to do it. Defending herself…"

"That's ridiculous. Why would she have a reason to pull a knife?"

She couldn't believe he was serious. "Could be a lot of reasons that have nothing to do with her being a danger. That could very well have been the only way she could defend herself. She's a girl in a system that doesn't listen to her or work. You really think a girl like her can just call for help and someone is going to listen? And don't forget that she's not white, so the average cop isn't going to waste a tank of gas or put any effort into finding her. There are too many strikes against her."

She wasn't sure what to make of the way he was shaking his head. "This file is troubling," she continued. "She's being bounced around, labeled aggressive, angry. Her foster parents couldn't manage her? I'd really love to sit down with her. Thirteen and already lost… And, what's worse, I can understand why."

She let the words hang as Mark drove up and parked outside the main cabin. She could see kids inside. He turned off the engine, and she pulled on the door, but he reached over and touched her arm. There was just something about his hand on her. Her gaze went right there, right to it, until he pulled it away.

"You said you pulled a gun at a gas station at her age. You were robbing it?"

Right, her and her big mouth. She never slipped up like this.

"I was a foster kid—like Shay," she said. "The day I pulled that gun was the worst and best day of my life, because that was how I met my mom and dad. My dad was there. When I was arrested, he got me out, and the rest is history…"

She stepped out of his Jeep, because there was no

way in hell she was talking with him about so many things that, to this day, she hadn't shared with anyone.

As she stood there, and he climbed out of his side, she took in the two counselors stepping out of the main cabin, Jeannette and Todd.

This place just didn't sit right with her at all.

Chapter 7

"Look," Mark said. "I told you we just need a word with the girls who shared a room with Shay, and we need to see the room, as well."

"I thought we agreed when you came here earlier that it would be best not to sound the alarm," Todd said. "Next thing, she'll be yanked back into the state juvenile facility and locked up, and she'll have lost her chance to be here at this camp. Not every girl in the system gets to come here, and I'd hate to see her lose all the ground she's gained. As I said, she'll likely turn up soon…"

What was it about this guy, Todd? It was starting to sound as if he didn't want Mark looking for Shay, poking around, or asking any questions.

He found himself looking over to Billy Jo, who was standing with the other counselor, Jeanette. He was still bothered by everything she'd said about him, how she thought he worked, how he just didn't care.

He'd never ignored someone or not helped someone because of social status or skin color—but there were situations where people sounded the alarm when they shouldn't, and there were differences in how things were judged as a result.

"You know what, Todd?" he said. "You need to cut the crap right now. This has gone beyond that. I can understand cutting the girl a little slack, but you have no idea when she disappeared. Now, I want to talk to the girls she shares a room with, because right now, it's sounding as if you don't want me talking to them, and that has me wondering why. What are you hiding? Because this seems like you're hiding something. Are you hiding something, Todd, about a girl who's in the care of the state and who you're responsible for?"

His eyes widened, icy blue, and his face paled. "No! Oh my God, no. I'm not hiding anything. I've just worked with these kids, and once the alarm is sounded, you can't take it back. It's another strike in a system that works against them. Renee and Jada are her bunkmates, and they're in their cabin now. Let's go."

He started walking, and Mark followed, taking in Billy Jo, who was staring at them. He didn't know what to make of her or what she was thinking. He gestured to her.

"Well?" was all she said as she fell in beside him. He noticed that Jeanette walked back into the main cabin, where he knew the kitchen was. Inside, some kids were cleaning up the tables.

"Going to talk to her roommates in her cabin," he said. "About earlier, I want you to understand that if she were a white girl with a family, I still would've done the same thing."

Why was he bringing that up? He took in how short she was as they walked up the trail, following Todd to one of six small cabins.

"Detective, I very much doubt that. If her mom and dad were from some nice suburbia, with money behind them, and they called to tell you their white daughter was missing at a camp on the island, I guarantee you that not only would you be looking for her, but your chief would have canceled his day off and headed up the investigation. Search and rescue would also have been called in, and the entire community would have been recruited. Search parties would be combing the island. No expense would have been spared."

He started to shake his head.

"You can tell yourself you treat everyone equally and the same, but it doesn't make it true," she continued. "If you don't want to be honest about the problem, fine, but let's be honest here: There are two kinds of law enforcement in this country. It's all about us versus them. Whichever side you think you're on, somehow you've convinced yourself you're not biased and everything works the same, but you're telling yourself a big old lie. Maybe you sleep better by convincing yourself it's not true, but I'm not sure what's worse. Telling me you enforce the law equally only tells me you're lying to me, but it's worse if you really believe that lie. This girl, Shay, already knows what you won't admit. No one is looking for her. No one gives a shit about her. But you know what? I do."

They stopped outside a cabin. The door was open, and Todd was inside, and he could hear him talking.

There was something about Billy Jo. It seemed that every time she looked his way, he was positive she wanted to poke his eyes out. She just reminded him so much of every woman he'd ever had trouble with.

He gestured to the open door. "After you. You want to talk to the girls? Well, so do I."

At the same time, though, as he followed her in, he couldn't help wondering what her story was. She had robbed a gas station? She had been in the system? He wondered if that was why she was the way she was.

He took in the small cabin, with three sets of bunks, each with a sleeping bag on the bed and a duffle bag on the floor. There were two girls, one brown, one black, sitting there, listening to whatever Todd was saying. They had hoodies on over their camp T-shirts, and both wore blue jeans.

"This is the social worker and the detective here," Todd said. "They want to ask you a few questions about Shay…"

Mark stepped over to him and stopped in front of the girls. "Thanks, Todd, but we'll take it from here, if you don't mind," he said.

Todd didn't leave, though. He only moved over to the wall, and he didn't miss the way Billy Jo tracked him as if she'd already figured out what he was suspecting. Something just wasn't sitting right with him here.

"Hi, girls," he said. "Look, we just have a few questions for you about Shay. Either of you know where she is and why she left?"

Billy Jo was leaning against one of the bunks. Her dark blue outfit, as he thought about it, was the same as one his mom had. She also had a big baggy purse over her shoulder. The way she was looking at him, he couldn't shake the feeling that she expected him to completely screw this up.

The girls shrugged and looked over to Todd. Were

they seriously waiting for him to say it was okay for them to talk?

"Hey, Todd, do you mind stepping out and letting us talk to the girls alone?" Mark said.

Todd was leaning against the wall with his arms crossed. "Well, actually, I do. I'm responsible for these girls, and they are minors, after all…"

He could hear Billy Jo say something to the girls behind him.

"You know what, Todd?" Mark said. "I'm getting the distinct feeling that you don't want me talking to the girls. Are you hiding something here?"

Todd was already shaking his head and gestured toward him. "Look, Jeanette already mentioned the marks on Shay and the fact that she's missing, but let me be clear: Jada and Renee are minors, wards of the state. If they know something or did something to Shay or had a hand in something, them talking to you without a guardian present isn't going to happen. For all I know, they could say something, and you could twist it, and it could blow up on one of them. Next thing, they'll have more trouble, or charges or something will be filed against them to further screw up their lives. I will not see them railroaded."

Mark lifted his hand to Todd's shoulder and somehow moved him to the door, then took a step outside with him. Inside, Billy Jo and the girls were still talking. "You know what? That sounds reasonable. In fact, if Shay weren't missing, I'd agree. But there was something about the way the girls looked over at you, as if they needed your permission to talk, and that bothers me. I have to say, that kind of thing raises some red flags. Your explanation is plausible, but I'm not here to jam up anyone. I'm just trying to find a missing girl."

The shock on Todd's face seemed genuine, but was that because Mark was off base or because he'd figured out that Todd was somehow controlling what the girls were saying and to whom? Maybe they were scared of repercussions or something. Mark pulled his arms across his chest as Todd sputtered.

"You know what?" Todd said. "I think I'd better put a call in to my supervisor. I too have a boss to answer to. So how about this? I'll step away for about ten minutes, and you can wait here. And if you happen to step into the cabin and the girls happen to talk to you, well, I guess that would be a conversation I wasn't privy to, so you can't use it against them. Then, when I get back, it will be with my boss's orders that you're to talk to the girls only in my presence. Then we can have that kind of conversation. But, again, any questions you ask before then will have been asked without my knowledge."

Mark shrugged, taking in a man he now had a lot more questions about. "Sure, I'll wait here. Don't rush."

Then he watched as Todd walked away. If the man were genuinely here to protect those girls, why had he given in so easily and walked away? He really did have a lot of questions about this camp, about the counselor… and about Billy Jo.

He stepped back into the cabin.

The moment the girls saw him, they stopped talking. He looked over to Billy Jo, unable to shake the feeling that he was being seen as the enemy.

"Again, let's talk about Shay," he said. "You girls are the only other two in here, and you share this cabin with her."

This time, the girls looked to Billy Jo. Something about the motion was really beginning to piss him off. He angled his gaze right to the woman who had been a thorn in his side since she landed on this island.

"Renee and Jada, you were assigned to this cabin," she said. "You said you didn't know Shay before arriving here."

The girls were nodding.

"This is a three-week camp," she continued, "and you said everyone here is from a foster home or a juvenile facility?"

He wished someone had thought to fill him in more on the girls here, the kids.

The brown girl—he wasn't sure of her ethnicity—shrugged and said, "Everyone here is from all over. But most of us are from a state home. I know I had to earn points to be able to come, keep my nose clean. It was like a lottery in the home I'm at."

"Not me," the other girl said, jumping in. "My social worker offered a place for me here, so there was no way anyone else was getting my spot. You talk to anyone else, though, and some had to jump through hoops. Some were sent because they didn't want to be here. Shay, pretty sure she was one of them. She hated the outdoors, nature. She didn't want to be here."

"You're Jada?" Mark said.

The girl didn't pull her brown eyes from him, and there was no smile. "I'm Renee," she said. "She's Jada. If you'd paid attention, you'd have known that."

He didn't miss the tug at Billy Jo's lips, and he thought she was hiding a smile. Maybe she got off on this kind of thing.

"Let's keep this discussion to Shay, Jada," she said.

"This is Detective Friessen, and he's helping in the search. You said Shay hated the outdoors, that she wouldn't have gone out for a walk and gotten lost?"

The black girl, Jada, hadn't pulled her gaze from him, and he couldn't shake the feeling that she didn't trust him. "Not Shay," she said. "I told you already: We went to bed, and the lights were out. Curfew is ten. She was here then, but in the morning she wasn't. Jeanette came in and woke me, asking where Shay was. Her bed was made as if she hadn't even slept in it. That's all I know. She kept to herself, even in the cabin."

Maybe it was the way Renee was looking over to Jada, but it was as if she knew something or they were hiding something. Maybe separating these girls and having a talk with each would be a better idea.

"Okay, but what about the marks on her?" Mark said. "Was someone hurting her?"

There it was again, an exchange between the girls. They knew something.

"That's it," said Todd from the doorway. "Stop right now. I just got off the phone with my supervisor, and there are to be no more questions. You cannot talk to the girls. Ms. McCabe, I was just advised by my boss that you're to contact your supervisor, one Grant Webber…" He was holding a post-it note, reading the name, and then stepped over and held it up. "Because, evidently, the search for Shay is being called off."

"Excuse me?" Mark said. He turned to the guy and took a step toward him. There was something about his face now, the way he took them in with a confidence he hadn't had before. "Like hell! A girl is missing. I'm not shutting this down."

Todd pulled his arms over his chest and stepped

closer. "Well, I suggest you have a word with your chief, because as far as I've been told, she's now been listed as a runaway, and no active investigation is underway. The state, and this is coming word for word from my boss, is not wasting valuable resources on Shay Williams. Detective, Ms. McCabe." He gestured to the door.

Mark knew when he was being kicked out. He glanced down to Billy Jo, but the expression on her face showed the same fury he was feeling. She looked up to him, and he didn't like what he saw there. She strode past Todd and out the door, but Mark took one step and then another over to the counselor, stopped right in front of him, and angled his head.

"You know, I have the feeling something's going on, that someone's hiding something. When someone tells me to stop looking, to drop a lead or close a case, then I know I've stepped on some toes. Did I step on your toes, Todd?" He knew he sounded like an asshole, and he could see that the friendly good old boy vibe between them was long gone.

"Out, now!" was all Todd said. "Oh, and, Detective, do have a word with your chief, because as I understand it, he's about to clip your wings." Then he lifted his hand in a wave, wagging his fingers. "And a word of advice? Sometimes these kids aren't worth the effort."

Chapter 8

She didn't need to walk into the police station to know that everything Todd had said was completely fucked up. But it was correct, she realized, as she waited on hold with Grant after seeing his text about another case.

She realized no one was going to be looking for Shay, and she was sick over it.

No, she was furious.

She stood beside Mark's Jeep, which was parked beside her Corolla, and watched him through the window of the station, talking to a man she realized had to be the chief, who had evidently come in on his day off after all. He was older, bald, with a thick mustache. He was rounder in the middle but the same height as Mark, and all she could see was the chief talking and Mark saying not a word. He gave a shake of his head with a pissed-off expression.

Here she was, standing outside, feeling like an absolute idiot.

"Grant is still on the phone," said his secretary. "Do you want to keep holding?"

She just couldn't shake the feeling that next, she was going to say he was gone for the day and she'd give him the message. "Yes, I'm holding," she said. "Please put a note in front of him to tell him it's Billy Jo McCabe, and I'm calling regarding his text and the missing girl, Shay Williams."

"Yes, I did, but, as I said, he's on a very important call. Again, I can take a message…"

"No, no, and no. I'm holding. Tell him I'm holding for him. This is crazy, ridiculous. It's not lost on me that I'm calling his cell phone, yet he's forwarded me to reception. Why? Seriously, you can tell him that I know he's avoiding me."

"I can't tell him that," his secretary said. What was her name again, Ruth or Michele? "Oh, he's off the phone. It looks like he's leaving…"

"Run, Go after him," she said, not quite shouting but giving everything to the call. She didn't care who could see her. All she could feel was that she was about to be told to close a file when she had no intention of doing such a thing. There was silence, and she knew she was on hold again. She pulled her arm around her waist, leaning against her car and waiting.

"So sorry about that, Billy Jo," Grant said. "I didn't realize you were waiting on the other line."

For a second, she pulled the phone away and stared at it. Then she put it back to her ear. *Liar, liar!* And he had tossed his secretary under the bus.

"Well, I told your secretary to slide a note in front of you saying it was me, and she said she did, so you're saying she lied to me?"

There was silence on the other end.

"Mix-ups happen," he finally replied. "So what is this call regarding? Because I have a meeting." Now he sounded short.

"Well, funny thing. I'm at the wilderness camp about the missing girl, Shay Williams, and all of a sudden I'm being told by one of the counselors that his boss and you, as well, and even the chief of police here, are closing this case. She's being called a runaway, and no resources are going to be wasted on her. But the fact is that she's still missing, and there were apparent marks on her, as if someone had a go at her, and—"

"The case is closed, Billy Jo. I texted you already. Besides, it's out of my hands. When orders come down, that's it. You don't argue. Look, this is a tough job, and choices have to be made about who we save and who we can't. There are limited funds. We can't waste a ton of resources on one girl."

"You mean one black girl in a state juvenile facility?" she said, nearly cutting him off. She knew she was over-stepping by the way he breathed out sharply.

"Don't pull the race card on me. It's got nothing to do with that and everything to do with who she was. She's got a history of running, and the call's already been made. Close the file. Move on."

"And what about the marks on her? Someone hurt her," she snapped, wondering how this could happen. She hadn't become a social worker to play politics, but she couldn't shake the fact that she was feeling very much as if she were being handled.

"We know nothing about marks," he said. "We have no reports of that. Did you see marks on her?"

She lifted her gaze, seeing the door open, and there was Mark. He was staring right at her.

"No, I did not see any marks. If you recall, when you assigned me to the case, she was already missing. I remember quite clearly you telling me about the camp counselor raising the flag about marks on her, so local authorities were also notified, yet you still want to shut this down? I mean, she has to be here somewhere. It's an island."

Something about talking to a person who wasn't listening took her beyond her patience. She took the palm of her hand and smacked her forehead, then fisted it.

"It's shut down," Grant said. "Case closed. It's already been noted in the file that the girl is gone, a runaway. She likely hitched a ride with a local off the island. In the meantime, you've been sent some files of our cases there on the island to check into. Now I really have to go. Anything else?"

She wanted to argue with him, but she knew when she'd already lost. "Nope," was all she said.

"Go meet the chief, be nice, and we'll meet later in the week to go over those new cases," Grant said. Then he hung up.

She hadn't missed the fact that she'd just pissed off her boss.

The chief was now outside with Mark, coming her way, as she slid her cell phone into her purse. "So are you the little lady who's taking over for Paul Krantz?" he said.

Right, the old social worker she knew nothing about except that he'd retired or something. The chief evidently saw her as a little lady, and he smiled and held out his hand.

"Yes, I'm Billy Jo McCabe. Sorry, but I didn't know Paul. I was told by my boss to stop in and introduce myself, but the missing girl took precedence."

Mark turned his head away slightly, the edge of a smile touching his lips. Apparently, he was amused.

"Yes, well, as I understand it, the case has been closed," the chief said. "I was telling my detective here that in the event any evidence surfaces pointing to foul play, we'll look at it, but until then, it's filed away. I understand she's a runner, so she's likely gone looking for her people."

Billy Jo wasn't sure if she gasped or if it was just in her head. She dragged her gaze over to Mark, who said nothing, looking the other way as if he weren't even listening.

"Now, since you're new to the island, the wife and I will have to have you over for dinner to welcome you." He reached over and patted her arm, offering a smile. "Mark, remember what I said—and don't forget your dog."

Then the man headed back into the police station.

A big dog, mixed breed, was wagging its tail, tongue panting, sitting next to Mark. She took in the long-haired mutt, and he just stared down at the dog and said nothing.

"So that's it, then," she said. "Case closed. It's that easy, huh?"

Maybe she just wanted someone to take this out on, but the face he made was anything but impressed.

"No, it's not that easy," he said. "You know, what I can't figure out is that just this morning, there was a big push to find the girl. Even I thought she probably went out for a walk, a hike, got lost. I had all those questions, you know, that should've been answered. But it's not lost on me that the moment we started pursuing the marks on her, wanting to talk to the other kids, good old Todd made one call and it was shut down. In this entire case, not even twenty-four hours have passed. Don't you find that odd? I mean, your boss and my boss tell us to, so we're filing her away as a runner?" He glanced down to the dog.

Billy Jo didn't know what to say to the guy who had been a big source of grief for her since she'd landed on the island. She wondered where, exactly, he stood on this. "So I take it you're not buying it, either."

He said nothing at first, then, "In all the time I've done this job, I've never seen anything put to bed so quickly before. I mean, the girl's still missing, right?"

She only nodded and pulled her arms across her chest.

"Only one way on and off the island." He gestured over to where she knew the ferry was.

"And she supposedly has marks on her."

He looked down at her with those brilliant blue eyes. "Seems strange to me, almost as if someone doesn't want us looking for her, and that just doesn't sit right with me. Right now, I just can't shake the feeling that someone's hiding something. Someone's messing with a kid and trying to handle us, and that…" He lifted his finger in the air as if to make a point. "That is just something I won't tolerate."

She pulled in a breath. "What, exactly, are you saying?"

He glanced down to his dog again and then back up

to her. "I'm saying my chief may have said the case is closed, but the case is closed when I say it is. Right now, a girl is missing. Someone doesn't want us asking too many questions, and I want to know who that someone is."

It took her another second to realize what he was saying. "So does this mean…?"

"Yeah. We're looking into this missing girl. Unless you're planning on listening to your boss and filing this away?"

What was it about this cop? She could feel that he tested boundaries and authority.

"Nope," she said. "I got into this business to help kids like Shay, so I have no intention of moving on. So what do you suggest, Detective?"

He jutted his chin to the hotel and bar across the road, close to the ferry. "Let's start over there." He started walking, and the dog fell in behind him.

"To look for Shay?"

He glanced back to her. "No, to grab a bite to eat, dinner, a drink. I'm hungry. Then we'll compare notes."

He was still walking, and she wondered whether, like the dog, she was expected to just follow him. She dragged her gaze back to the police station, seeing the chief through the window, on the phone, looking at her and Mark.

She took in her car, which was still locked, and Mark, who was already across the road, and she crossed the street after him.

———————————

Chapter 9

———————————

"Mark, how many times have we told you to leave that dog at home?" the owner of the Wheelhouse said as he filled Mark's coffee mug—which, Billy Jo noted, had come with a shot of whiskey on the side, which he'd poured in.

She was at an outside table, sitting across from him as he dug into his steak.

"Can't," he said. "He's not my dog."

She thought he was kidding, but the owner just shook his head. She took him in, an older guy with dark hair and glasses. She wondered how well they knew each other.

"He looks like your dog, Mark," the man said. "Follows you everywhere, so seems he's decided he's yours. Just saying, at this time of year, some of the visitors don't like seeing dogs in restaurants where they're eating."

Mark was cutting a few pieces of steak to put on a side plate, which he leaned down and gave to the dog. Billy Jo forked up her pasta and shrimp and took in the detective across from her, whom she couldn't believe she was basically breaking bread with.

"He's a stray," Mark said. "Been on this island longer than me. Just because he follows me around, doesn't mean he's my dog, Pete. You should know that."

She didn't know why he was arguing about it. She wondered whether this was something he did all the time as she took in Pete's expression.

He shook his head and looked over to her. "How is everything?"

She had been about to take a mouthful when he asked. "It's good. Thank you."

He offered her a smile before dragging his gaze back over to Mark, who had an odd smile, and then down to the dog, who was licking the plate.

"So the dog is a stray," Billy Jo said, "but you're feeding it, and it follows you everywhere, and it's not your dog?"

He cut another big piece of steak and shoved it in his mouth. "That sounds about right," he said as he chewed it.

She took in the dog, who had finished the meat and was now lying at his feet. "So whose dog is he?"

Mark just shrugged. "No idea. He just showed up one day and wouldn't leave."

"Hey, you two!" came a voice from the table across from them. "Remember me from the ferry? Nora."

There was the blonde, in a blue and white tank top with a matching skirt, sunglasses on top of her head. Pete put a menu in front of her, and she offered a bright smile before he walked away.

"Right, the party girl who was looking for fun on the island," Mark said.

Billy Jo wondered whether he talked to everyone that way. She took a bite of her pasta, seeing the blonde still had her eye on him. She actually wrinkled her nose, her smile big, bold, vibrant.

"Oh, you make me sound just horrible," she said. "No, I'm here visiting. It's called a vacation, relaxing—you know, that thing you take to recharge before going back to your crazy busy city life? Now, I didn't know you two knew each other!" She gestured to them.

Billy Jo was about to say they didn't when Mark gestured to her with his fork and said, "Eat up. As soon as I'm done, we have to go."

"Anyway, it's such a small world, isn't it?" Nora said. "You're a cop, right? You must have all kinds of stories about crazy things that happen on an island like this. Kind of like this morning, when that crazed gunman was shooting things up and you took off up there to protect all of us."

Billy Jo nearly choked on her mouthful of pasta. The woman was so shameless in her flirting that for a moment, she was almost embarrassed. Mark didn't seem affected at all, though. He probably heard it all the time.

"Yeah, that was weird," he said, then turned to Billy Jo. "Got up there and CJ wasn't even around."

"Anyway," Nora said, "what a beautiful place this is! Didn't get to see it all, but I have a hike planned for tomorrow. There are these two wineries here I wanted to try out, and I signed up for kayak lessons. Then there's whale watching. Did you know you can even rent a boat and drive around the island? There's just so much to do here. Why, I'm green with jealousy that you get to live here year-round and do all this for fun. I should actually consider moving here."

Pete arrived with a glass of wine and slid it in front of her. She was still talking, Billy Jo realized, but now to him.

"So," she said, turning to Mark, "you haven't shared too much about what your chief said to you."

Mark just shrugged and looked over at her. "You didn't share what yours said to you, either. I'm thinking it was the same, that we're meant to shut it down. We don't want to ruffle feathers. She'll likely turn up when she's arrested for shoplifting or something. Sound about right?" There was an edge of sarcasm to his voice.

She shoved another mouthful of pasta in her mouth.

"So," Nora cut in again, "what do the locals do around here for fun at night? Any nightclubs or places to go dancing or anything like that?" She rested her elbow on the table, her chin in her palm, and gave everything to Mark. Her smile was stunning.

"Locals have dinner and are in bed by nine," he said. "Generally, we're up at dawn. So the only nuisance people at night here are the visitors. The locals are at home."

He turned back to Billy Jo, and she shoved the last shrimp in her mouth as he cut up the rest of his steak to give to the dog. He wiped his mouth with a napkin, likely waiting for Billy Jo to say something in response, but she realized she was in that silent place she went when she was furious.

"Pretty much the same message I got," she finally said, "though not in the same words. My boss was trying to blow me off, doing his very best to avoid having an actual conversation with me." She shrugged.

Mark laughed. "Yeah, I can see that. I don't think I'd want to get on your bad side," he said. He shook his head as if considering something. That was just some-thing she was starting to pick up on from him: He seemed to consider things in silence.

"But, you know," Billy Jo said, "you said something before about her going for a hike or a walk and getting lost. I don't know about any of that. I'm not getting the sense she'd do something like that, not from what I read in her file. And when I was in the cabin, talking to the girls while you were outside with Todd, they said that right from the beginning, Shay was off. She kept to herself, didn't want to hang with any of the kids there. They said Todd had more than a few conversations alone with her, yet I'm pretty sure he failed to mention any of that…"

She could feel Nora watching them, and she put down her fork and rested her napkin on her plate. Mark leaned back in his chair, shaking his head. At least he hadn't told her to get lost and drop the case. She could be thankful for that much.

She watched him lift his coffee and take a big swal-low, then reach into his pocket and pull out his phone. She hadn't heard it ding, but it must have, as he looked at the screen and swore under his breath before shoving it back in his pocket.

"Shit," he said. "Okay, we've got to go." He stood up and pulled out his wallet to toss some bills on the table, and as she shoved back her chair, reached for her purse, and unzipped it, he just waved his hand and said, "I've got this." He whistled, and the dog got up.

Nora was watching him walk away. "Hey, it was great seeing you again," she called out, lifting her hand to his back.

Billy Jo only nodded before hurrying to catch up to

him as he walked out of the hotel restaurant, the white two-story building on the harbor. He stopped right at the road and shoved his sunglasses on, as the evening sun was right in their eyes.

"Come on, what's going on?" She reached out to touch his arm before he started walking again. She was very aware the dog was right there.

"Couple of fishermen found a body. Pulled up their crab pot and thought it was snagged on something, but it turned out it was a teenaged girl."

Her heart sank. "You think it's her, don't you? Shay."

He waited until a pickup drove past, then started across the road, and she fell in beside him. "Maybe. I can honestly tell you that the only missing teenager we have is Shay Williams, but do I want it to be her? Hell no. At the same time, whoever she is, she is someone's daughter."

Mark hurried to his Jeep, then glanced back once to her and called out, "Come on, hurry up."

All she could do was nod, because she suddenly realized that she'd been completely off base about him. Just maybe, he really did have a beating heart and cared about what had happened to Shay.

Chapter 10

He knew the chief was already there as he climbed out of his Jeep and snapped his fingers to the dog, then pointed sharply and said, "Stay."

The dog lay down in the back, and Billy Jo stepped out of the passenger side. The sun was sitting just at the edge of the horizon, with only moments before darkness set in.

He took in the chief's car, with the Roche Harbor Police logo in blue with a gold star emblem, and he could feel his anger building with each step as he took in the scene ahead. A single boat was tied to the public dock, and four people were standing on the rocky shore, their backs to him.

Billy Jo said nothing as she fell in beside him. Mark lifted his sunglasses and settled them in his hair on top of his head.

His chief turned to him in a dark blue police jacket and ball cap, his expression grim. He held up a hand to Billy Jo and said, "You don't want to see this, little lady."

"Actually, I do, Chief—and the name is Billy Jo, not little lady, if it's all the same to you."

Mark didn't have to look over to see how pissed she was. At the same time, he knew when his chief would stand his ground, so he said, "It's fine. Let her see. Anyone ID her yet?"

The medical examiner, Odo Voight, stood nearby. He was also the part-time local doctor, and Mark had heard he'd delivered most of the kids born on the island up until ten years earlier. "No, she's pretty messed up," he said, just standing there and looking over to the two men who had found her.

Mark had seen them in town a few times before. They were standing with Carmen Zarco, one of the deputies, who'd been on the job for nearly eight years, her dark hair tucked under a ball cap, in uniform. He could hear her sharp tone. He knew nothing about her other than that she was single and loved peanuts and cheap beer. He'd heard she had a kid somewhere who didn't live with her.

He didn't have to look up to know that Billy Jo was right there, and so was the chief. "You know what happened to her? Cause of death?"

The tarp was pulled back, and he took in the sightless eyes, the marks on her dirty clothes. He was sure it was Shay. He wondered if this was something he'd ever get used to. He had to lift his gaze, wondering if the image would ever go away. Billy Jo ran the other way, and he could hear her vomiting off to the side.

"Hard to say, really," Odo said, then jutted his chin to where Billy Jo had run off. "Is she going to be okay?"

The girl was still uncovered, and he took in her shirt,

the short sleeves and shorts, everything gray. From what he could see of her legs, it looked like she'd been bitten. She wore a belly button ring.

He slid his gaze over to the chief, who shook his head, then lifted his brows as he glanced over his shoulder to where Billy Jo was. He wondered whether he'd say, "I told you so." Mark chanced a glance, seeing her bent over at the knees as she puked.

"Guess now we know it's probably best if she stays behind a desk," the chief said.

Mark didn't miss the slight, and for a moment, he had to wonder if the chief had always been like this. He said nothing, remembering the first time he'd puked and nearly passed out after finding an old woman who'd been stuffed in a trunk by her grandson.

He waited for the ME to stand. Odo's hair was thick and curly, going white in places. He was a short man, at least six inches shorter than him. The body was still uncovered.

"Those cuts on her…" Mark gestured to her arms, her legs.

"Post mortem," Odo said. "Some are likely from the lines she got tangled in. A few crab pots were down there, and she was hooked onto one. Those guys didn't realize it was a body they were yanking on, pulling up their crab pot. They likely tore her up a bit. Some, though, appear to be cuts from a knife—from before. Seems she was worked over. I would put her at fifteen, sixteen, maybe. No ID. From the marks on her neck, it looks like she was strangled. You can tell by the eyes. There likely won't be any evidence on her, from how long she was out there. I would say foul play. She was dumped, by the looks of it. Don't think she was meant to be found," he added, and Mark wondered how he could stare at the girl, at her dead body, and not be affected.

"How do you figure that?" the chief said.

Odo dragged his gaze over to them and then squatted down. He pulled the tarp all the way off to reveal a rope around her ankle, cut off at the end.

"She was weighted down," the chief said, turning to Mark, his hands shoved in his jacket pockets. "When she was pulled up, the rope was tied to an anchor. The boys over there had to cut it to get her up. The anchor is still down there."

Mark just shook his head and dragged his hand over his face. "So this missing person's case, Shay Williams, is now a murder investigation. Who had you shut this down, again?"

By the expression on his chief's face and the way he took a step closer, he thought he was going to rest a hand on his shoulder to set him straight, but he just said, "The chain of command is just that. When an order comes down, you follow it. You may not like the decision, and there have been many over the years that I've wanted to question, but you don't get to. I've been doing this for a long time, Mark, and we don't have a bottomless cup of money."

He was still waiting for the chief to tell him who it was. The mayor, the council, someone at the county? The chain of command had a lot of people, a lot of positions, and a ton of politics. He just shook his head.

"Get her back to your office, Doc," the chief said. "If you need to call in help, let me know. I'll have to have a word with the county."

Odo went to cover the body back up, but Mark looked again at the clothes, the shorts, the T-shirt. Something about this didn't sit right with him.

"She's barefoot," he said. "Odo, is this all she had on?"

"This is it. The two who pulled her out brought her in like this, in their tarp, as well. We just need to get an ID on her."

Mark nodded, feeling the eeriness in the scene. This was a nice rocky beach that people walked down with their kids, yet here was a kid who wouldn't see another birthday.

He walked over to Billy Jo, who was now standing up. He could see how pale she was even with the night settling in. "You okay over here?" he said.

"Fine," she bit out, though he didn't miss the shaky breath she pulled in.

"So I guess this changes things," he said. "A murder investigation… It looks like she was strangled, and the body was weighted down. Someone didn't want her found. I mean, how the hell did she get all the way out here? She was at the camp. Now I'm thinking Todd knows way more than he's letting on. It's time to sit him down and have a chat. And Jeanette, too. Who was the boss he called, and who did your boss talk to? The big question I have is why we were told to stop looking. Who wanted us to stop?"

He realized Billy Jo wasn't looking his way. She'd said nothing. Maybe she was more rattled than he thought, as she pulled in a breath and then another one.

"This the first dead body you've seen?" he said.

She pulled her arms over her chest and then spat on the ground again, shaking her head.

"We need to get a positive ID on her for the record."

"You'd think after everything I've seen, I wouldn't be bothered by seeing that girl lying there like that," she said. "I've seen a lot of things—horrible, awful things. I've never even told my parents everything. I think my dad knows some things, though. You know, being in the system and getting bounced around, I know well the kinds of things the kids at that camp see, the kinds of things they shouldn't have to know at their age.

"They know no one really sees them for who they are. No one really cares about them, not the way a parent does, or a family, the way you should be cared about. You learn early on that the only one you can count on is you. It's a lonely existence, and you start to shut down. You tell yourself it's better that way. Trusting anyone is a mistake, so you don't do it.

"The thing is that you learn it early on, a painful lesson, because as soon as an adult says, 'Trust me, it's going to be okay, don't worry,' you know every one of those words is a lie. You should worry, you shouldn't trust, because you'll be gutted when you're ripped from the one family you thought maybe, just maybe, might want to keep you, or you're put somewhere where you have to sleep with one eye open and a knife under your pillow, or you're accused of something and no one believes you didn't do it."

Why was it that he couldn't shake the feeling that she wasn't talking about Shay? It was more personal. He'd never had to worry about anything like that. Having Jed and Diana Friessen as his parents, he'd never known anything but love.

"You think you're up to IDing her?" he said. "Then

I think we're done here, and this becomes a murder investigation, so——"

"It's not her," she said, looking up at him. She ran her hands down her front as if smoothing out her shirt.

He just stared at her. "Excuse me? Of course it is. She's black, about the right age. There are no other kids missing."

Billy Jo was shaking her head. "No. I got enough of a look, and it's not Shay Williams. Shay is thirteen, and she's a black girl. That girl is brown, likely native—you know, from one of the local First Nations? And she's older than Shay. I saw Shay's photo and what she looks like."

"Well, maybe the photo isn't recent. Did you think of that?"

Billy Jo crossed her arms over her chest, and the way she looked at him, he could feel the argument coming. "Then how do you explain the skin color? That girl isn't black. She's from one of the local tribes. There's a difference."

She turned and lifted her hand toward the chief. "That's not Shay Williams, so you'll need to ID her," she called out.

Mark didn't have to look over to his boss to know that he wasn't going to take her word for it. He wanted this case closed, and Mark wondered if he'd just put Shay Williams's name on the deceased girl.

Billy Jo was already walking back over to the body, to the chief, to the ME. "I don't know who that girl is, but she's not Shay Williams," she said. "It seems she's still missing, and now you have the body of another girl. Seems to me, if I were you, that this kind of complicates things. You sure you still want to close the Williams case, Chief? Because if you have dead girls being weighted down in the ocean, it sounds like maybe you have more of a problem here. What do you think would happen if the media were to find out? 'Local chief shuts down search for a missing girl, and another is found murdered.' I'm pretty sure that could hurt tourism and have a spotlight shining on you."

He couldn't believe she'd said that!

The chief pulled in a breath in a way that told Mark he was about to lose it. Then he made a rude sound and said, "You threatening me there, girl?"

Mark took one step and then another over to the chief, seeing that Billy Jo wasn't about to back down. She stood her ground, and Mark stepped in between them. "Chief, she's right, and you know it," he said.

The chief nodded, then gave a shake of his head. "You want to keep looking, be my guest, but on your time, not the county's. And her—you keep her on a short leash."

Then the chief walked away.

Mark dragged his gaze over and down to her. "Word of advice, Billy Jo: Alienating the chief here isn't going to win you any points. In fact, if you lock horns with him, I guarantee you he can make everything here very difficult."

She only nodded. "You think he's the first asshole I've had to deal with? I get it, but I'm also not going to kiss his ass. I'm sure you can do that," she said. Then she started walking back to his Jeep.

Carmen, the deputy who had been questioning the fishermen, stepped up beside him. Evidently, she'd heard everything, and as she watched Billy Jo walk away, she said, "You know what? I like her."

He looked down at the deputy he barely knew, then back to Billy Jo. "Yeah, well, don't go telling her, but maybe I do as well."

Chapter 11

"You really think we'll get any answers tonight?" Billy Jo said.

The dog was leaning over her seat and panting. His breath was bad, he was drooling on her shoulder, and she was about to sneeze, as he was also shedding. Detective Mark Friessen seemed to have only two ways to drive, fast and faster, over dark, narrow roads with a few ruts here and there. Her hand was on the dash, and her purse was on the now cleared floor. She could hear the old takeout packaging rustling in the back.

"We'll get something," he said. "I'm not leaving until Todd answers my questions."

There was something about this detective. He was so damn serious and focused. She wondered what his story was.

"I never asked you back at the beach, where that girl's body was, if this kind of thing happens often here. I mean, I've been here not even one day, trying to find a missing girl, when another one turns up dead."

He didn't say anything. What was he thinking?

He pulled back into the camp, where the only light came from the cabins. There was just something about this place: It seemed a person could slip in at night and not be found.

"Not like this," he said. "Stuff happens, a few unsolved cases, but not like this." He shook his head.

He drove up the hill and parked right in front of the main cabin, and she could see the counselors inside with the kids. Mark pulled up the emergency brake, then had the engine off and was out his door at the same time she was. In the chill of the night, she wished she had a sweater to pull on.

"Detective, Ms. McCabe. You heard," said Todd from the wooden porch. A single bulb served as the outside light, and she wasn't sure what to make of his expression. Inside, she heard talking, kids' voices.

"Heard what?" Mark said as he walked around the Jeep, the dog still inside, while Billy Jo said nothing.

"Well, that Shay came back," Todd said.

Mark rested his hand on the front of the Jeep. He didn't look over to her, and she found herself wondering what he was thinking.

"Where is she?" Billy Jo said. "What happened?"

Todd was still looking at Mark, and something passed between them. She wondered for a moment whether he would answer her, but then he looked right at her.

"Seems, like I said from the start, that she went for a hike, got lost, and found her way back."

If Billy Jo was good at one thing, it was knowing when something was off—and something about this was definitely off. "Huh," she said. "Well, there's still the matter of the marks on her. I'll need to see her and speak with her."

She dragged her gaze over to Mark, who only nodded. He seemed to be thinking heavy thoughts. She'd have loved to pull him aside right now.

Todd was shaking his head. "I'm not sure that's a good idea. She's in her cabin, likely asleep. It'll have to wait until the morning..."

"No, it won't wait," Mark said, stepping forward. "She was missing. You say she was on a hike and got lost? I guess we'll need to hear it from her, make sure she's okay." He brushed his jean jacket back, and she knew his badge was right there.

The screen door to the main cabin opened. Jeannette, the one counselor she knew was on Shay's side, stepped out with a small milk and fruit cup in one hand, a flashlight in the other. "You heard she's back? Walked right in here," she said with a bright smile.

Todd was still standing there, and he gestured toward her. "I was just telling the detective that Shay is exhausted and is in her cabin, asleep."

"No, she's not," Jeanette said. "I just came up to get this for her. She's hungry. She was taking a shower." She stepped off the deck. "Come on. I'll take you to her, and you can see she's fine."

Billy Jo shrugged.

Mark lingered in front of Todd for a moment, then dragged his gaze over to her. "Go ahead. I'll catch up," was all he said.

"Okay," she replied, then fell in beside Jeanette, wondering what Mark was saying to Todd.

"I know I really pushed the panic button," Jeanette said, "and maybe Todd was right that I overreacted, but

I just really care about these kids, and I couldn't help fearing the worst."

Something about Jeannette was so nice, she thought.

"Don't worry about it," Billy Jo said. "I'm just glad she turned up and nothing bad happened to her. It's the kind of happy ending I want to see. But, when she got back, did she ever say anything about what happened? Then there are the marks. You said someone was hurting her?"

Ahead, soft light poured through the screen door of the cabin. She didn't hear any voices.

"I don't know," Jeanette said. "When she just disappeared, I may have overreacted about that as well. I hate to say this, and don't tell Todd, but I think he may have been right. She may have hurt herself." She stepped up on the wooden porch and pulled open the door. "Shay, I grabbed you a snack."

Billy Jo followed Jeanette in the cabin, seeing only Shay, her dark hair sticking up everywhere, sitting on a red sleeping bag in her bunk, wearing gray pajamas with a dark hoodie pulled overtop. No one else was there.

She looked around and let her gaze land on Shay, who was now holding the small carton of milk and the fruit cup. "Hi, Shay," she said. "I'm Billy Jo. I'm a social worker. I was sent up here earlier when you disappeared, I was worried something had happened to you. So you went for a hike?"

She took in a bag beside the bunk, beside which was a pair of sneakers, neat and tidy.

"That's right," Shay said. "It was silly. I just wanted to be alone."

Billy Jo didn't miss how she had glanced at Jeanette before looking back over to her. "Well, what time did you head out? Because I understand you were gone when Renee and Jada woke up. They said you hadn't even slept in your bed."

Shay said nothing, staring at her with the kind of look Billy Jo knew all too well. She was untrusting, and could she blame her? No.

"Yeah, I guess that's right," Shay said. "Look, I'm tired. Is that all?" She glanced back over to Jeannette again.

Billy Jo knew she wasn't going to get much from her.

"Yeah, we should really let her get some sleep," Jeanette said.

But something about all of this didn't sit right. Billy Jo had an unsettled feeling she couldn't shake. Maybe it was from seeing that dead girl, though. "Well, I just wanted to ask you, too, about the marks on you. Is someone hurting you?"

There it was, the moment she pulled back. She knew that look well, considering she'd lived through these circumstances herself when she was Shay's age.

"No one hurt me," Shay said. "I fell."

Jeannette said nothing. She had expected her to add something, but she didn't.

"Fell, really?" Billy Jo said. "According to Jeanette, you had a fair bit of bruising. That could have been from someone kicking you, grabbing you, hurting you. You're saying that didn't happen?"

All she did was shake her head. "Nope, just clumsy, is all. If you don't mind, I'm tired. I'd like to go to sleep."

Right. Trust was essential, and there was no trust in Shay's expression.

"Sure, get some sleep," Jeannette said. She went to step away, and Billy Jo turned to her.

"Could you just give us a minute alone?" she said.

Jeanette seemed to consider it for a moment, then glanced back and over to Shay. Her gaze lingered on her until she finally said, "I'll be right outside, Shay." Then she stepped out.

Billy Jo waited until they were alone, listening to the screen door close. She stood right in front of the girl. "Just you and me, Shay. I know you don't know me and don't trust me. I can't blame you, but I'm telling you I'm here for you, and whatever you tell me stays between you and me. If someone is hurting you, I can help you."

Shay lifted her gaze to her. Her dark eyes, which should've been filled with light, were filled with the heaviness of having no hope. Billy Jo wondered whether her eyes had looked the same way when Chase found her. Maybe she should call her dad and mom and thank them again, or maybe just tell them how much she loved them.

"Excuse me, but you think I haven't heard that before?" Shay said. "I told you already: I fell. I'm clumsy. Is that all?"

No. Billy Jo wanted to ask her about her bunkmates, about where she'd really gone, about Todd, about the fact that she was lying to her.

But she said, "Yeah," and she reached into her bag to pull out one of her cards. She held it out to her. "Here's my card, Shay. For what it's worth, if you ever want to talk about anything, need help, or find yourself in trouble, call me anytime."

Shay just stared at the card. Instead of taking it, she just looked away, so Billy Jo bent down to her bag, where her shoes were, and tucked the card in one of them. She knew Shay was watching her, and Billy Jo let her gaze linger for a second, expecting her to reach out and rip the card up.

Then she stepped out of the cabin just as Mark approached, Jeanette still outside.

"She told you nothing," Jeanette said.

Billy Jo shook her head. "Nope. She closed up, not trusting. Can't blame her."

As she stepped down, Jeanette stayed there and nodded before saying, "I'll keep an eye on her."

Billy Jo took in the cabin, Jeannette, and the camp. She wondered why she didn't feel like this was a happy ending.

"Everything good here?" was all Mark said as she fell in beside him, walking back to his Jeep. Jeanette had gone back into the cabin.

"As good as it could be," she said.

"Yeah, well, at least she turned up."

She knew she nodded, but she couldn't sound happy. "Yeah, I guess that should be good news."

Mark said nothing. He pulled out his cell phone and flicked on the flashlight over the darkened ground.

"What did you talk to Todd about?" she said. Would he even answer her?

"Likely the same thing you talked to Shay about: what really happened." He walked up to the Jeep, to the passenger door, and pulled it open for her.

"Did you learn anything?" She stopped in the open door as the dog poked its head out.

Mark rested his hand on the frame and seemed to look past her into the darkness. "Only the same things you probably did. She went for a walk, got lost. No one's telling the truth."

"You ever feel like we walked into the middle of something?"

For a moment, from the way he stared down at her, she wondered whether he'd call her crazy. Then he glanced away and said, "Maybe. Hard to say. At least she's here." Then he gestured for her to get in. "Any plans this Friday night, your first night here on the island?"

She pictured the red wine in her fridge, the chocolate brownies she knew her mom would've sent, and this detective, whom she couldn't figure out. "Put my feet up, hang with my cat, and try to forget this day. You heading back to work?"

He looked away and then behind him. Something about the motion told her he had something on his mind. "Tomorrow," he said. "Seems one case is solved, but now another is open." Then he looked back to her. Something about Detective Mark Friessen seemed complicated and difficult.

Instead of saying anything else, she climbed in. He closed her door, and she glanced back to the dog and said, "So you like him, do you?"

The dog licked her face in response as Mark opened his door and climbed in. He glanced at her and the dog and only grunted before starting his Jeep and backing out, driving out of the camp. She couldn't help but think that maybe he wasn't quite the arrogant jerk she'd first thought.

"You like what you see?" he said.

Ah, there he was.

"You go out of your way to be an asshole, don't you?" she said.

He smiled as he kept driving. "It's a talent I have."

She just shook her head as she looked straight ahead. "Evidently, Detective."

———————————————

Chapter 12

———————————————

He'd made a pot of coffee, and he reached for the bottle of whiskey, which was half empty, and poured in a splash as he took in the mutt softly snoring on the old leather sofa by the window. His cabin was small, one bedroom, but it was private and quiet, and the only thing he heard at night was the waves crashing against the shore to lull him to sleep.

His cell phone was ringing, and as he took in the number and name, he couldn't keep the smile from touching his lips. He answered and pressed the speaker. "Hi, Mom. Like clockwork, you are. I swear I could set a watch by when you call."

"Hi, Mark," said Diana. "You know, you said you would call this week, and I didn't hear from you, so here I am. Is it too much to ask that you pick up the phone and call your mother, your father? We miss you, you know, and it's been ages since we've seen you."

He tapped the spoon after stirring his coffee and lifted the mug, then took a swallow, loving the taste. It was his favorite drink, with the warmth of the whiskey at night. "I know," he said. "I would have called, but it was kind of a hairy day. You know crime doesn't take a holiday."

He picked up his phone and walked over to the sofa to sit down beside the dog. He wondered whether he should figure out a name for the mutt.

"What happened?" she said. "Can you talk about it?"

He just shrugged, thinking of Shay having turned up, his conversation with Todd, which had gone nowhere, and Jane Doe, who was now on a slab. His boss had texted him an hour earlier to say that case would go to the Feds.

He thought, too, of the woman he'd spent most of the day with, who hadn't made anything easy.

"Not really," he said. "A girl went missing and then turned up."

And another was found dead. He pictured the closed file.

"Well, that's good news! So let me guess: You're sitting home alone on a Friday night."

He knew where this was going. He reached over and rubbed the dog, who was sleeping contently. "I'm relaxing at home after a long day."

"You need to get out and meet a nice girl."

He lifted his gaze to the ceiling, knowing his mom wouldn't be happy until he got married, just like his two brothers, Danny and Chris. "I thought you wanted me to be happy."

His mom made a rude noise on the other end. "Oh, Mark. One day. Speaking of which, your dad was talking to your uncle Neil. He said the niece of a good friend of his has taken a job on the island as a social worker. You should reach out to her."

He took another swallow, staring at the phone, which was still on speaker. He set it on the coffee table. "Let me guess: Her name is Billy Jo McCabe?"

It seemed it was rather a small world at times.

"I take it you met her. So did you hit it off? It would be nice to know that you're looking in on her, too. Is she a nice girl?"

He knew what his mom was doing, and he shook his head. "Oh, we hit it off, all right—like gasoline and firecrackers. She's mouthy and bossy, she argues endlessly, she's difficult…" He stopped talking, as there was silence on the other end.

"Wow," Diana finally said. "Sounds like you met your match."

He rolled his eyes even though he knew his mom couldn't see him. "That's not funny, Mom. Listen, do you know anything about her? She mentioned something about being adopted, and I think she may have been in the system a while. She said something about robbing a gas station, and I'm thinking she may have had some other troubles." He didn't know why he was asking, but everything about Billy Jo McCabe seemed to be a mystery.

"Well, I do know she was arrested. She pulled a gun at a gas station, and your uncle's friend's brother, a lawyer, got her out and then adopted her. Heard she had a rough time. I have to tell you, Mark, although you and your brothers never had that kind of worry, I did. It's not something I talk about. The system isn't known for turning out well-adjusted kids, but at the same time, I think your uncle would appreciate it if you kept an eye out for her, make sure she's okay, check in on her."

He stared at the phone. "I'm not dating her, Mom."

"Who said anything about dating? I just said to look in on her, be nice to her."

"Okay, Mom, I'll keep an eye out—but, and I hate to tell you this, I'm pretty sure Billy Jo McCabe can look after herself. Anyway, tell me about everyone else at home. How're my big brothers, Dad, my nieces?"

He leaned back on the sofa and took a swallow of his coffee, listening to his mom talk about his brothers, his family.

He couldn't help wondering what Billy Jo McCabe was doing right now. What, exactly, was her story?

Maybe one day, he'd find out.

Chapter 13

er shoes were clean.

Billy Jo bolted upright in bed. Her cat, Harley, who had been sleeping on her chest, let out a meow of disgust as he hopped around and tried to resettle himself. She rested her hand on him, realizing now what had bothered her the night before: Shay said she'd gotten lost in the woods on a hike, but her shoes were too clean. No, she knew she was being lied to.

The fact that Shay had been found should've been enough. But it wasn't, not by a long shot, because Shay's expression the night before had been something Billy Jo would never forget. For a moment, she had felt as if she were looking backwards in time at herself at that age, when she'd hated everyone and trusted no one.

Her hand went right to her cell phone. She took in the chief's number and kept scrolling until she landed on Grant. She listened to the ring of his cell: one, two…

"Hello, this is Grant." There was an echo in the background.

"Grant, it's Billy Jo. I want to talk with you about Shay Williams, and—"

"The case is closed," Grant said. "We had this discussion yesterday. I understand the girl is back now, just gone for a hike. Well, with the alarm having been sounded, she's being sent to a high-risk state facility."

Billy Jo tossed back the covers, and Harley lifted his head, looking so put out, his eyes barely open. "You mean locked up like a criminal? Yeah, I know what high risk means. You think that's fair?"

She heard the sigh on the other end. She had never expected it would be this difficult. As someone who understood all the closed doors and roadblocks these kids faced, she hadn't expected to be playing the same game she had when she'd been just a kid, without a voice in the system.

"It's got nothing to do with fair and everything to do with how this works," Grant said. "She didn't have permission to leave. She caused a lot of unnecessary worry, and don't forget the resources that were wasted on her. That's money the county won't recoup."

She wanted to bang her head against the wall, because she was talking to Grant the bureaucrat right now, not Grant the social worker, who was supposed to give a shit about this kid. She squeezed the phone. "I thought being a social worker meant helping kids, being a voice for Shay and others like her."

She could almost hear her dad in her ear along with the sizzle of the burning bridge.

"There are protocols and rules in place for a reason, Billy Jo," Grant said. "For the most part, they work. So what is this really about? Because we already discussed this. Close the file and move on. You have other cases, and if Shay wants things to work in her favor, she needs to follow the rules and cooperate."

She wanted to scream. She shook her head. "Grant, I spoke with Shay last night, and I'm telling you, something doesn't add up."

"I guess you didn't hear me. The file is closed—or are you determined to waste more resources? Because I have to tell you, Billy Jo, your job isn't to play detective and create a problem where there isn't one. The report I have on file says she was having a disagreement with the girls she bunked with and took off when she should've reported any problems or incidents for the counsellors to handle. Is there anything else?"

She started out of her bedroom in just a nightshirt, seeing the open bottle of red wine, the half-eaten tray of brownies, and the sun just coming up on the horizon. "What about the marks on her? You were the one who notified me, remember. It was in her file. One of the counsellors at the camp reported it."

She heard him pull in a breath, but it was one she recognized, one that said he had already stopped listening and now was just plain annoyed.

"Billy Jo, let me give you some friendly advice," he said. "If you want to last in this career, you need to be able to close the file and walk away, or you'll burn out. You can't get emotionally attached, because the job will rip your heart out, and this is from someone who's been at it as long as I have. Sometimes you have to look at the best-case scenario, and we're there. About the marks, I understand she explained that she fell, or rather, she probably hurt herself. I've seen these kids do all kinds of things for attention."

She realized he wasn't going to hear her.

"Anyway, if I recall correctly, this is the weekend," he continued, "so you should be unpacking, getting ready for another week with other cases, and familiarizing yourself with the island, maybe seeing the sights. Heard they have great kayaking and hiking. Be a tourist for the day. Again, you'll burn out if you start taking it too far. All you need to do is look into it and see that the kids are sheltered and have food and a bed. Remember, too, that these kids know how to mess with you and read any weakness in you. Now, I have a golf game scheduled in an hour. How about you don't call me again this weekend unless it's an emergency?"

Then he hung up.

She held her cell phone out, staring at it. Something about this situation still didn't sit right with her at all, because she'd lived through the same things Shay had, and she remembered well that the system hadn't been there for her and hadn't believed her.

She thumbed through her contacts again and hovered over the chief's name, then Detective Friessen's. For a moment, she wondered what she was thinking. The detective was a jerk, impossible.

She held the phone up, listening to the ring.

"What!" he snapped in answer.

"Detective Friessen, this is Billy Jo McCabe."

"I know who it is."

Okay, she could add rudeness to his list of qualities. "Great, then you should know that I don't believe Shay went for a hike and got lost. In fact, I don't believe she was out in the woods at all."

There was silence for a moment.

"Detective, are you still there?"

"Yeah," he said. "Yeah, look, she likely wasn't—but she's back, so is this still an open case you're investigating?"

What had her boss said? Case closed. But instead she replied, "When we were there last night, her shoes were too clean."

Again, he said nothing for a second, and she wondered whether he realized she hadn't answered his question.

"What do clean shoes have to do with anything?" he finally said.

She actually rolled her eyes. After all, he was the detective, but here she was, picking up on the problem. "If she went for a hike and was gone for that long, lost, walking around, her shoes wouldn't have been as clean as they were. I mean, even in dry weather like this, I'd expect caked-on dirt and debris. Let me ask you, how are the trails? I don't think it's been that long since it rained." She knew she was reaching.

He said nothing for another second. "Okay, fine, I'll give you that. Let's say she wasn't out hiking, lost. Then where was she?"

That was the million-dollar question.

"I guess that's what I would like to know," Billy Jo said. "As for those marks on her, the ones she said she got from falling, she's now being scheduled to be sent to some high-risk facility. Remember how we were both shut down? Then there's the girl who was found in the ocean, dead…"

"You're not trying to link the two, are you? Because there's no evidence of that."

She shrugged, spotting the French press and the

kettle. She lifted the small bag of coffee beside it. "I'm just saying there are questions that still need answered. Although Shay has been found, I really believe something happened to her. I know last night she didn't believe anyone was out to help her. I was staring down into distrust, and I understand well that she's scared, because someone did something. Whoever it is, she's likely trying to look after herself, because word will get back to that person. She knows she won't be believed, and what will happen to her at the hands of whoever is hurting her could be far worse."

He sighed on the other end. "Fine. Give me half an hour."

She stared at her closed front door. "Half an hour for what?"

"You said this is still open. The girl's in trouble. I'm on my way over to pick you up."

"And go where?"

"You have questions, and the girl's lying, so we'll go back to the camp, talk to her again, and get the truth out of her. I don't know. It's called investigating."

She ran her hand over her bed hair, still needing to shower, get dressed, and have coffee. "Oh, wait. You don't know where I live."

"Yeah, I do," he said. "You seem to forget I'm a detective. Be ready."

Then he hung up, and she took in her cat, who was now hopping out of the bedroom. She quickly filled the kettle and plugged it in, then raced into the bathroom to grab a quick shower.

She suddenly had an unlikely ally, but she knew she was stepping on toes.

Then again, she would never sit back and say nothing just because she might upset someone or rock the boat. Stepping on toes and rattling cages was what she did.

Chapter 14

"You know, how about I drive today?" Billy Jo said. She was in a pair of red capris, flat sandals, a white T-shirt, and sunglasses and was holding a go-mug, which he hoped held coffee. She stood with the door to her Corolla open after he'd circled around and pulled up beside her, rolling down his window and resting his arm on the frame as he kept the clutch in, the brake on, and the Jeep idling. He wondered why she was smiling.

"How about you not?" he said.

Her smile left.

The last thing he wanted was to have to sit in the passenger side of any car driven by a woman—any woman. He had things to do, and the last thing he wanted was to explain his reasons for doing the things he did and going the places he wanted to go.

"Are you seriously going to go all caveman and insist you be the only one to drive?" she said.

Was she really arguing? He pulled his sunglasses down just a bit and stared at her, then at her coffee, which he'd not had nearly enough of. "You want to find out about this girl? Then get in."

She firmed her lips, reached into her car for her baggy purse, looped it over her shoulder, and gave her door a shove closed before starting around his Jeep.

She took in his floor, which had only one takeout cup, tossed there from the coffee he had finished a moment earlier, and she reached for it and tossed it in the back before climbing in. When she'd closed the door, he put it in gear and started driving.

"Where's your dog?" she said. He wasn't sure what to make of her expression or the way she'd asked. He thought of the dog, who had showed up one day and had never left.

"He's not my dog—and he was sleeping on my sofa when I left."

There it was, that something. He didn't think she could smile.

"I didn't think your boss would be interested in pursuing anything," he said. "Even the chief made it clear to me that this was a closed case. So what are your theories on what happened?"

She'd fastened her seatbelt, her go-mug between her legs. He made no attempt to drive around the ruts in the road, and as she bounced in her seat, she lifted her mug and took a swallow.

"I don't know," she said. "But I was that kid, and the last person I would've talked to was someone like me or you. Seriously, any time people said they were there for me or would help me, I had learned it was a lie. I was the one dealing with the fallout of what really happened behind closed doors. There's no one to call for help, because no one will believe you. But they will believe the supposed adult who has been entrusted with your care, because that's the way it works.

"I never could understand how the benefit was always given to the foster parents, to those in authority, and the onus was on me to prove they were lying. They could spin a lie about me or put something in my file that wasn't true, and there was nothing I could do about it. The way Shay looked at me last night, I knew she didn't believe a word I said. It felt like lip service, saying those things we were taught to say. Of course she's not going to just come out and say someone hurt her or something happened, because what she knows is that in the system, everything she says will go right back to whoever hurt her, and that person will get the benefit of the doubt.

"Whoever it is could say she lied and it didn't happen, or she did something instead. Someone could make up all kinds of things, and people will believe the adults who are supposedly looking after her. Whatever they do to her behind closed doors, she'll have learned long ago not to talk about it."

"Are you talking about the foster system, her foster parents?" Mark said. "They can't be all bad. You make it sound like everyone is out to make her life miserable."

She didn't shake her head, but she made a rude noise. "No, not everyone, but unfortunately the system has a lot of bad in it—bad foster parents who were never properly vetted, in it for the easy cash. Those kinds of people hurt kids, ignore problems. Then there are those facilities, the high-risk places, which are basically jails. Shay knows well that the only way to survive there is to keep your head down and ignore everything. There are always worse things going on there, and although the people running those institutions know it, they say they don't. So her response last night wasn't unexpected."

"Is that what happened to you?" he said. When she hesitated, he wondered whether she'd answer.

"Oh, me? I was running because I knew I wouldn't survive where I was. I was looking for my mother, determined to find her. Then everything went sideways, and I met my dad, my parents, who adopted me. I was lucky." She breathed out, and there was just something in her expression that he couldn't put his finger on. "I don't want Shay to have to live in the kind of fear I did, the kind of fear where she knows no one gives a shit about her or cares about her or is looking out for her. Whoever's hurting her, I want it to stop. I want her to know that I can fix it for her and that she can trust me, and whatever she tells me isn't going back to the person who's hurting her. Because you know what happens then?" She turned toward him.

He already had an idea what she meant. "You mean you're worried about giving whoever this is a heads-up so that they can retaliate, get their story straight, and spin it back on her."

She looked at him, unsmiling, as he pulled into the camp again, seeing the activity, the cars and kids. Something was going on. As he pulled in and parked, he realized that just maybe they could slip in and talk to Shay before Todd and Jeanette realized they were there.

Billy Jo, who had been quiet while he parked, said, "Yeah, well, I also want to talk to Renee and Jada, because I swear they know something. There's no such thing as a kid keeping her nose down and not knowing anything. They know exactly what's going on; they just don't have an incentive to talk."

She pulled open her door and stepped out, and he followed her around the Jeep in his faded blue jeans and jean jacket. Kids were walking into the main cabin, some to other cabins, and there were adults there too, as if this were an open house or something.

"So, let me ask you, how do you get one of these kids to talk if she doesn't trust you?" Mark said.

Billy Jo pulled off her sunglasses and slipped them on top of her head even though the sun was out and bright. "Well, I can tell her again that whatever she says, I won't share it, but I guarantee you she won't believe me. I'll figure it out. The only way the girls will talk is if they believe I really have their backs, that I've got something to give them, a new place to live or something that will make them believe life could be better for them. Hey, that's Jada, Renee, and Shay." She gestured to the three girls, who were walking from what he thought were the showers back to their cabin.

He reached over and touched Billy Jo's arm. "Hey, just wait a second. What's the plan? We have to have one before we go in there. And what about Todd and Jeannette? Maybe I should let them know."

She just shook her head. "No. How about we have a talk with the girls without Jeannette or Todd, no one there to shut this down on us? Then the girls won't be able to check to see if it's okay that they talk. Todd knows something, and so does Jeanette, and those girls didn't want to talk to us with them in the room. I want to find out why."

He looked over his shoulder to the main cabin, expecting to see the counsellors or someone chasing them down to ask why they were there. Then he started after Billy Jo down the path through the trees to the girls' cabin. She tapped on the screen door, and he could hear their voices inside.

When she opened the screen and stepped inside, he didn't know why, but he couldn't shake the feeling that something just didn't seem right. He followed Billy Jo in, letting the door close quietly behind him, and he took in three sets of eyes now staring at him. By their expressions, he realized that what Billy Jo had said about these girls was right. The way they were staring over to him, it was as if he were the enemy.

"Hey, girls," he said. "So how about we discuss what's really going on here? Where were you, Shay, really? And, Jada and Renee, you can tell me exactly why you lied to us."

Billy Jo dragged her gaze over to him. Of course, she hadn't expected him to say that.

"Don't know what you're talking about," Renee said.

"I thought you were going to let me handle this," Billy Jo said, her voice low, as she stepped over to him.

He pulled his arms across his chest, taking in these tough-as-nails girls, whom he figured he wouldn't be able to reason with. "We don't have that kind of time," he said, "so this is how it's going to work. Jada, Renee, Shay, you're going to tell us everything. Who's hurting you, Shay, and why is it that every time Todd or Jeannette is here, it seems as if you're following a script that's been dictated to you? If you don't start telling the truth about what's really going on, the next place you live is going to make your current facility look like a walk in the park, and the hell you think you're living in will only get that much worse."

Chapter 15

Hadn't he heard a word she'd said?

Billy Jo couldn't remember the last time someone had yanked the rug out from under her so hard. She stepped over to Mark, so close to him, looking up at him and seeing his sunglasses nestled in his red hair. His arms were crossed, and the seams of his worn jean jacket were pulled tight.

"What are you doing?" She kept her voice low and leaned in, hoping he felt the bite of her words.

He didn't pull his gaze from the girls. She could see the tough love in the way he was looking over to them. It was the same kind of stand her dad had taken with her a time or two, and she'd never liked it. Then he flicked his gaze down to her for only a second and said, "Not coddling them."

He stepped around her over to the girls, who she could see were likely too shocked to say a word. "I believe I asked you something. The first person who speaks is getting a bus ticket to wherever she wants to go or a say in where she wants to live next—and, believe me, I can make something happen."

Was he crazy? She reached for his arm and felt solid muscle, and he only glanced down to her before she let her hand fall away. How had she ever thought she could reason with this man?

"Come on, you three," he said. "Clock's ticking. Or is it that all of you are living in such wonderful places now that nothing could be better, and you're dying to get back? Shay, I understand you were living in a nice, cozy Leavenworth youth detention facility with barbed wire and locked doors, but you're now headed to iron bars, crowded bunkrooms, group showers, and the kind of guards who will hurt you and take advantage of you in jail until you're eighteen. You thought it was rough before? It's going to get worse, and you know why? Because you're not speaking up.

"You continue to spin this lie about taking a hike and getting lost. You're giving someone the power to use your problems as leverage. When you don't speak up, when you don't fight back, it becomes permanent. I mean, who came up with this story about a hike? And, Renee and Jada, which facility do you call home? How many homes have you lived in with a locked door, wanting something better? You have to want something. Come on, seriously, what do you want?"

Billy Jo just stared in horror, unable to figure out why he was doing this. At the same time, she could see the hesitation in the girls' expressions, the way they weren't looking at one another to decide what to say. Would it be another lie or the truth? She didn't know. It could be anything to survive.

"An honest-to-goodness bus ticket anywhere?" Shay said. "You're not messing with me, are you?"

Billy Jo couldn't pull her gaze from Shay, because the girl was actually considering it. "Detective, what are you doing? She's only thirteen," she whispered to him, but she knew the girls could hear.

He didn't shrug. He said nothing as he glanced back to her for only a second. "You think shoving her in jail is any better than giving her the chance to go somewhere else? I also said, Shay, that I can find you someplace better to live, too. It's your choice. The bus ticket gets you to a new place, but you're still only thirteen, and that sucks big time, because you'll likely be picked up and tossed into another system somewhere else, or you'll be right back here or off to someplace worse all because some adult gets to decide what's best for you. I can find you someplace better. Maybe there is one."

"I have a sister, a twin sister," Shay said. "I haven't seen her in ten years. I don't know where she is. I want to see her. Can you make that happen?"

Billy Jo now couldn't pull her gaze from Shay, who was standing with her arms crossed in a hoodie. She took in the scar below her eye, then glanced back to Mark.

"I'll find her," he said. "I'll make it happen."

"How do I know you're not lying?"

"He's not lying," Billy Jo cut in. "I won't let him."

He didn't smile, but there was something in his expression. She didn't have a clue what he was thinking, and that scared the hell out of her. "No, Shay, I'm not lying," he said. "I know you were born in Tallahassee, and you have a twin sister, Shauna, who's in New Mexico with the family that adopted her. Your mother,

Desiree, was shot and killed by a cop. They said it was self-defense, that she was running away and refused to stop, that she was going to pull a gun. She reached for something in her pocket, and the cop fired his gun four times into her. She was dead before she hit the ground.

"It was her ID she was reaching for. You and your sister, who were only three, were sitting in an old car in the parking lot, waiting for her. You saw everything. The cop was never charged, and your mom had no one to claim her body. She was buried by the city in an unmarked grave. I read it all, even the cop's version about a suspected robbery, suspected drug possession, how she wouldn't stop when ordered to. The cop panicked, but what happened would never have happened to someone who wasn't black. I get it, Shay. I would be furious, too. Then there's your dad."

What the hell was he doing? Shay's brows knitted with confusion, because her father's identity was unknown. Billy Jo had already told Mark that. Where had he gotten all this information from? She was racking her brain, because what she'd read in her file only skirted over what he'd said. This was the kind of blindside she hadn't felt in years, and she didn't much like it now.

"What are you doing, Mark?" she said, but he only shook his head.

"Look, this girl has been lied to her entire life, separated from her sister," he said to her before turning back to Shay. "Your father was in the army. He didn't know about you or your sister."

"You're lying to me," she said.

Mark was still shaking his head. Where the hell was he getting this? Even she didn't have access to this kind of information. She tapped his arm again, but he only tossed her an unreadable glance. He was messing with Shay, and this was the kind of thing he couldn't do to a kid like her.

"No, it's the truth," he said. "Shay, your father was listed on a sealed hospital record I found. His name is Trent Jefferson. He's retired from the army and owns a tire shop in Kansas."

She stared at him as he stopped talking. Billy Jo wondered how and when he'd found this out.

"Girls go missing all the time, and no one looks for them," Shay said. Renee and Jada were looking at her with shock, surprise, betrayal—all three, maybe.

"Is that what happened?" Mark asked.

Billy Jo spotted something in the exchange between the girls. *Holy shit!*

"I was coming out of the shower, going to bed," Shay said, "and someone came up behind me. A hand went over my mouth. He was big, a man. I couldn't scream. He covered my nose, and I couldn't breathe. He was so strong. Then he had me face down on the ground. Someone else put a blindfold on me and duct-taped my mouth and my wrists. My ankles were zip-tied. I was put in the trunk of a car and taken to a house somewhere on the island. It was big, but I remember a gate, because I heard the electric motor when it opened. I was carried in over the guy's shoulder down some stairs, outside, and into a basement, a locked room. The door was steel, and the floor was concrete. There was another girl there. Bri was her name. I've never seen her before…"

"Who was it who took you?" Mark said.

Billy Jo just stared. By the way Renee and Jada were

watching Shay, Billy Jo realized they hadn't known everything. Secrets and lies and more secrets... She had a sick feeling about where this was going.

"I don't know who grabbed me or who owned the house. I know it was a big place. I only heard voices. When the man who had grabbed me tossed me over his shoulder, I heard music and voices like at one of those backyard parties, and what sounded like a pool, splashing... You're sure you're not messing with me about my sister and that bus ticket?"

At the way Shay said it, Billy Jo thought she might kill Mark herself if he was lying.

"Shay, you just say the word, and we're out of here," Mark said. "Renee and Jada, you two know something? Because I'm pretty sure you said you saw her at, what was it, curfew? That was at ten. You said the lights were out and she was here. Why'd you girls lie?"

The girls seemed to freeze, and she recognized those tight-lipped expressions she was staring at. She'd mastered it well herself at that age.

"So who at the camp was a part of it?" he said. "Was it Todd?"

Something about hearing his name and knowing that a counsellor could be behind this made her sick. At the same time, it shouldn't have surprised her. She had known something was off with him.

"You think Todd is behind someone taking me?" Shay said, then shook her head. "You want me to talk any more, I want to see that ticket first, because if I talk about the kind of people you want me to talk about, I know I'll never see the light of day otherwise. They're bad people. I know I would've disappeared. I may be only thirteen, but I know I was being sold."

Billy Jo realized that what Shay was feeling, the fear in these girls, was something she'd known well.

"You give us a name, Shay, and I'll have you out of here, all three of you," Mark said. "I'll put you in the back of my Jeep, and we'll drive out of here. You'll get protection, and I swear no one will get their hands on you. They were trafficking you and the other girl, too?"

She'd known they were scared before, but with Mark saying what he'd just said… A sex trafficking ring, here? He had to be wrong.

Renee forced herself to swallow and then nodded. "It was Jeannette who told us we were to say we saw Shay here at bed check. She said she didn't want to see Shay written up. I didn't want to say it, and I think she knew, because she said I had to or she'd write us up, saying we threatened her, stole something, or—"

"And you believed her," Mark cut in.

For a moment, as she tried to take in what she was hearing, Billy Jo was starting to put together a puzzle that left her with a sick feeling in her stomach. "Has she written you up before?" she said, realizing Mark didn't believe the girls.

Jada had a pissed-off expression. Billy Jo was trying to remember what she had read about her from her file. Which First Nation was she from? The Sioux, from the reservation in South Dakota, yanked from her home and community when she was two. Somehow, she'd ended up out here. Jada made a rude noise, dragging her gaze from Billy Jo to Mark, and shook her head. Was she going to answer?

"They don't like the way you look at them," she said. "If you look at them sideways, or you look them in the eye when you should be looking down, or you give them attitude of any kind, you get written up and lose all privileges. They tell you the way something is, or how you saw something, and those had better be the same words that pass your lips. Yeah, I was stashing puddings, taking two at dinner and putting one in my pocket. Todd found them, took them, and wrote me up. I lost dessert privileges for the rest of the time here and was put on duty cleaning the outhouse. I was hungry, is all."

Right, Billy Jo thought. Law and order were everything when running a camp like this, but she remembered reading in Jada's file that she often stashed all kinds of things.

Shay lifted her gaze to Mark and then to her—and just then, the screen door opened. She turned to see Todd in the doorway, his expression furious.

"What the hell is going on here?" he demanded.

"They just showed up here and threatened us," Renee cried out.

Todd took a step closer to them. "I'm calling the police," he said, his cell phone to his ear.

"I am the police on this island," Mark said, "and if I were you, I'd hang that up right now. What I want to know is if you're part of this trafficking ring. It's the perfect cover, really—this camp for troubled youth in care. I mean, who's going to miss one when she disappears? No one, especially if the file already says she's a runner. Close it and move on. What I can't figure out is how Shay came back, and why. She was gone, taken. You tossed all these obstacles in our path, with your calls to your boss, and then everyone wanted it shut down, or was that you? Why report her missing at all?"

Todd stilled. She swore he couldn't have looked more surprised. "Trafficking?" he said. His voice sounded off. They had all his attention before he dragged his gaze back over to the girls and said, "Is this true?"

As he took a step toward them, she could see the freak-out the girls shared: Tell the truth or lie? Lying would protect them, whereas the truth could have them disappearing tomorrow.

"By God, someone had better start talking and telling the truth," Todd said. "Did you not go for a hike and get lost?" He took a step closer to Shay, and Jada and Renee seemed to step away from each other. Yeah, she could see the self-preservation, the fear.

"Todd, I need you to step away from the girls," Billy Jo said. "You're scaring them. We're leaving with them."

Todd dragged his gaze over to her, then to Mark, and then shook his head. "No, you're not. No one's going anywhere until someone tells me what's really going on here," he said, the demand clear in his tone.

"Jeannette was there," Shay cut in, and everyone stilled. "And she was talking to another woman."

"Jeanette, from this camp, was where you were held?" Billy Jo said, because for a moment, she thought they were talking about someone else.

Shay glanced once at Todd and then over at Mark. She was scared, hesitant. Words were unlikely to follow.

"Shay, come on," Billy Jo said. "I know exactly what you're thinking, because I was your age once, sitting in a jail cell, about to go down for something. If it hadn't been for the man who saved my ass and then adopted me, and me having the courage to trust him, I wouldn't be here now. So when I say you can trust me, I'm not lying to you. I know you've been lied to, and adults you should have been able to trust have turned their backs on you. Please, are you saying what I think you're saying?"

For a second, she still didn't think she'd answer.

Mark, who was right beside her, said, "Come on, Shay. Billy Jo is right. You've got to trust someone here. Are you saying you heard Jeanette at the house where you were held, locked in a room? Are you saying Jeannette was there?"

Shay swallowed, staring long and hard at Todd, and then she nodded. "It was the other woman who said there was a buyer for us. They were taking us on a boat to Vancouver. Because they'd lost one, I was the replacement. But there was no way I was going."

She dragged her gaze over to Mark, not sure what she was seeing in his expression. "And you didn't see them," she said.

"I heard them talking outside the door. All I heard was Jeanette calling her Nora. They were laughing about some distraction, some timely explosion or something that pulled everyone's attention away, someplace by the ferry."

Under his breath, Mark swore and said, "At CJ's! Damn, and he wasn't even there."

Billy Jo was still stuck on something else Shay had said. "Did you see the other woman, the one Jeanette called Nora?"

Shay shook her head. "I didn't see anyone. I was blindfolded. I just heard her laugh and the way she talked about us, like we fit an order."

"How did you get away?" Mark asked. "You just walked back here?"

Billy Jo wanted to pull him aside. Nora! And he had to have an idea about the house, too. But Mark was right. Had they just let her go? Had they just let her walk out of there?

Shay said nothing for a second, then, "I heard a cell phone ringing, and then Jeanette was talking to someone. Whoever was on the other end told her to let me go. I don't know why. Soon, I was tied up again, blindfolded, back in the trunk. They let me go at the end of the trail behind the camp and told me to walk back."

"And, let me guess, you were told to say you were on a hike and got lost?" Todd finally jumped in. Billy Jo could see how rattled he was.

"I was told not to ever talk about what happened—or I would find myself locked up in a place where nightmares are made."

Yet here she was, talking. Billy Jo dragged her gaze back up to Mark. She didn't have a clue what he was thinking.

He looked over to Todd. "Where is Jeanette now?"

The man was rattled, in over his head. Todd swore softly under his breath, pulled his hands through his hair, turned in a circle, and then dropped them to his sides. "She left at dawn, the first ferry off the island. So now what?"

What was it about Shay now? She seemed to be breathing easier.

"About this Nora," Billy Jo said. "Shay, would you know her voice if you heard her again?"

Mark was looking right at her, and she could see he didn't get it.

"Nora, the blonde from the ferry, remember?" she said, gesturing.

"You sure that was her name?"

She nodded. "I never forget a name. It could be a

coincidence…" she said, but as soon as she did, it didn't feel right.

Shay was staring, wide eyed, from her to Mark. Then she shrugged. "Yeah, I'd know her voice if I heard it."

Mark just stared down at her, long and hard. "Well, then I guess we'd best locate this Nora," he said. Then he looked back over to Shay. "And then, for you, I have a promise to fulfill."

Chapter 16

"You have to have an idea where this house is," Billy Jo said. "I mean, how many houses on the island have a pool?"

Mark was still trying to get his head around the story he'd just heard. He couldn't remember ever feeling the chill he did now. How could something like that happen here? The island seemed welcoming, yet he knew a lot of things went on behind the scenes, hidden. After all, he had come up against closed-mouthed locals every now and again.

"Detective, are you going to answer me?"

He looked across the hood of his Jeep to the young woman, freckles spattered over her nose and cheeks, whom his mother had asked him to keep an eye on. She was far from helpless, though. She could look after herself.

"Do you ever get the feeling we're being played?" he said.

The way her blue eyes stared at him, he could see

she didn't get it. "In what way, exactly? I seriously hope you're not implying that Shay is lying to us."

He could see that she was totally in the girl's corner, yet something about it all still didn't sit right with him. He got a feeling when he knew someone was good for something and when a story was being spun.

"Just hear me out before going all overprotective mama bear and shutting down," he said. "I need you to really listen to what I'm trying to say."

There it was, that sharp look he'd wondered whether he'd ever get used to. She crossed her arms, still standing on the other side of the Jeep, and didn't pull her gaze. "You didn't answer me about Shay," she said. "You think she's lying. Are you about to go back on the promise you made? Though, by the way, let me point out that you giving a thirteen-year-old in the system a bus ticket to anywhere isn't going to happen."

Of course, she was right about that—but he had never said the bus ticket wouldn't include having someone on the other side, waiting for her.

"I'm not often wrong about things," Mark said, "but I have to say that I may have been wrong about Todd. Seems he may have been played, too. But how didn't he have an idea something was going on under his nose?" He shook his head.

No, he had to wonder, because hadn't the girls mentioned him having conversations with Shay in private? What exactly had that all been about?

"But to answer your question about the pool, the house," Mark said, "the fact is that Shay didn't see where it was, and on this island, there are a lot of really big, expensive homes with pools. There's money here, a lot of money. Unless something more is provided, we can't show up at every house with a pool. We'd never get a search warrant here, because the people who own those pools are judges, politicians, and the kind of people who donate enough to the governor to shut us down with one phone call. Then I'll likely be stuck giving out parking tickets or something in another county.

"We need a lot more. What this sounds like is a trafficking ring, sex trafficking, which is one of the least pursued crimes in this country. The investigations are underfunded. The number of girls who disappear only to never be seen again… Task forces don't exist for this, though they should. Yeah, I believe she was taken. But, knowing it's happening here, right under my nose on this island, I believe someone else here must know about it, too."

The chief? he thought. *Maybe.*

"But you know what?" he continued. "I'm having trouble with the fact that they just let her go. There's no way they would let her go that easy. Something is going on, and I think somehow we're being played as pawns to clean up some mess."

As he stopped talking, Billy Jo was watching him, considering something.

"Let me ask you, Billy Jo, you really think they would let her go just to walk back in here and tell us what happened, to give us Jeanette, to toss out the name Nora? I'm still having a hard time getting my head around that, because what I'm hearing is that the blonde showed up on the island to…what, take girls away, meet up with whoever is holding them? I don't buy it.

"It's more likely that wherever this house is, there's a private dock with a boat where the girls would be smuggled out to a Vancouver port, onto a shipping container, and transported somewhere to never be seen again. Years later, they'll show up on the streets, if they show up at all. But why give up these two women, and why this camp? This doesn't make sense. These rings are not small time. They have a lot of people making them work. But yeah, I'm not a total dumbass. I know girls in the system are easy prey. Look how easy it was to shut our investigation down."

He could see activity, Todd walking out of the cabin and back to the main lodge. The questions continued to plague him: Who was Todd's boss? Who had called his chief? Whose hand had tried to shut this down? This was bigger than them. If he were smart, he would take the small win, Jeanette and Nora, and close it up and move on. But Mark had never taken the easy way on anything.

"Okay," Billy Jo said, as if she had an idea of what he was thinking. "I'll give you that much. Maybe it seems too easy. But are you saying Jeanette isn't involved? What do you suggest? Do you think the body of the girl who was pulled up is connected?"

This really was a gorgeous piece of property. He took it in, the perfect place to help some kids—until one disappeared.

"Don't you?" he replied.

His cell phone starting ringing, and he pulled it from his jean jacket pocket. The warmth of the day was starting to rise. He stared at the screen, seeing the chief's name.

"The chief," was all he said before pressing the green answer button. "Mark here."

As he looked up, Shay was walking their way with a backpack, ready to climb into his Jeep.

"Where are you?" the chief said. "Got a call. Seems you may have been right about something being off at that camp. Seems one of the counsellors has been arrested, and I've got some Feds showing up in the next bit. Get in here now."

Mark pulled his hand over his head and didn't look away from Billy Jo as he said, "On my way." He hung up just as Shay drew closer. He could see the other girls in the distance.

"Well?" Billy Jo said. "What did he want?"

He inclined his head. "To say I was right, and now it's been solved. Someone's been arrested. Or maybe I'm totally wrong. Either way, it likely won't be anything I expect." He tapped the hood of the Jeep and took in Shay, who was staring at him from where she stood beside Billy Jo.

"You know, one thing you never cleared up, Shay, is the marks on you," Mark said. "You said Jeanette was the one behind this, yet she's the one who reported you missing, reported the possible abuse. Maybe you could shine a light on that."

All he got was silence before Shay said, "Is this where you tell me the deal's off?"

He dragged his gaze back over to Billy Jo, who he could see, just maybe, was now on the same page as him. He shook his head. "When I give my word, Shay, I mean what I say. But at the same time, if you aren't being straight with me, our agreement will start to fall apart."

She looked at him and then shrugged. "I told you the truth."

He expected Billy Jo to say something else, as she just stared at Shay, but all she did was pull in a breath, look back over to him, and say, "Well, let's go, then."

Chapter 17

"Close the door, Mark," said the chief, sitting behind his desk.

Mark glanced at the dark-haired man who lingered in the corner. He wore black jeans and a dress shirt, too clean cut to be an average cop.

"This is Special Agent Ramirez," the chief said, gesturing toward him. It wasn't lost on Mark that he hadn't taken off his ball cap, which he usually did inside. Mark could see that something wasn't sitting right with his chief, who clearly knew a lot that he didn't.

"Detective," Ramirez replied as Mark shook his hand.

Mark just glanced back to Billy Jo and Shay waiting in the bullpen by his desk. Whatever they were discussing, it appeared Billy Jo was doing all the talking.

"It seems you may have been right about the situation at the camp," the chief said. "The Feds here have apparently been monitoring a situation—which, to be clear, I had no knowledge of. I'll let Agent Ramirez fill you in."

"That's right, Detective," Ramirez said. "We've been monitoring a ring trafficking young women. One of the counsellors at the wilderness camp was under surveillance for a while and has just been arrested for holding three girls here. She's already confessed. The body that was recovered was one of those girls, missing from the reservation in Olympia. The other one is already in protective custody. Then there is Shay Williams, who will be going to a secure facility."

He kept his arms crossed in front of him as he stared at the man. "Shay was kept at a house here on the island, so I'm having a hard time believing it was just Jeanette."

The agent nodded, and from the glance he exchanged with the chief, Mark realized something else was going on.

The chief tapped his pen and said, "We already know about the house. It was a vacation rental, leased to Jeanette, and we understand she had a partner, Nora Cassberger, who was playing tourist. She's already been picked up and is in custody with the Feds. That young girl, Shay, is going to be accompanying the Feds now. They have questions to ask her, and this mess is now off my island." He swept his hand across his desk.

"So Shay was really being held with another girl at the house?" Mark said. "What about the men, the people there? She heard voices and was carried by a man. Are you really trying to tell me that two women, one a camp counsellor, working for the state, were trafficking girls?"

The agent didn't pull his gaze. "Nora and Jeannette are by no means the masterminds behind this. There are many more up the chain, and yes, this goes much bigger than two women running things. But this is what we have now, and we'll be taking Miss Williams off your hands." Ramirez jutted his chin toward the bullpen.

Mark glanced back to see two other men, Feds, he thought, standing with Billy Jo and Shay. The girl yelled, and one of them grabbed her and pulled her away. Billy Jo was cussing.

Yes, he'd just been played.

"So you basically knew I was bringing her in," Mark said. "You were just waiting."

The agent only shifted his gaze to the chief, who looked down at his desk, tapping a card.

The chief didn't get up from his chair as he said, "Mark, some things are out of my hands, and this is one of them."

Agent Ramirez straightened from where he had been leaning and walked over the door behind Mark, then pulled it open. "Again, Chief, thank you. We'll be in touch," he said. Then he stepped out.

Mark could see the fury in Billy Jo's expression, in her eyes. She was arguing with one of the agents, although he couldn't make out what she was saying.

"So that's it, to hell with Shay?" Mark said. "I made a promise to that girl to get her to talk, and it didn't include being passed over to the Feds and locked up someplace."

The chief flicked his gaze up to him and then stood. The way he looked across to him, Mark could feel the heavy hand of the law. "You know how this works, Mark. The Feds come in with more jurisdiction and take over. We have no say. The girl will be fine. At least she isn't in some container, being shipped off and trafficked, never to be seen again. She got a break. Sometimes making those kinds of promises is what you have to do to get them to talk, but you can't always keep your word, not in this business. Let yourself off the hook."

He knew arguing would get him nowhere. He watched as the agents left, and it was just Billy Jo standing there, nothing calm about her.

"You know, Chief, this seems too simple, too neat and tidy, how it all fell into place," Mark said. "When you shut this case down when Shay disappeared, who called you?"

The chief said nothing as Mark rested his hand on the door. The way he pulled in a breath and looked down, he wondered whether he'd answer him. Then he looked straight at him and said, "Take a few days off, Mark. Get your head straight. Calls come in all the time. I have to answer to the state, to the county. I don't get to question it. But sometimes, with a case like this one, it is that simple. Sometimes you start seeing sharks where there are just fish."

The chief didn't say anything else, so Mark pulled open the door and stepped out, right into the fury being directed his way.

"Mark, what the hell is going on?" Billy Jo said. "Who were those men who took Shay?"

He gestured to the door, said, "Let's go," and stepped out of the station.

Billy Jo followed.

At his Jeep, he pulled his keys from his pocket and stopping by his door. "It seems the case is closed. Those were federal agents, waiting for us. Seems Shay has answers they want, and our wings have just been clipped. Do you want to grab a drink?"

Her eyes widened as she glanced across the road to

the hotel. "Mark, it's still morning, not even noon yet. The bars aren't even open."

"Who said anything about a bar?"

She glanced back over to him. "Fine, where?"

He pulled open the door of his Jeep. "Get in, because I know the perfect quiet spot. I don't know, Billy Jo. It feels like this isn't the outcome we wanted."

As he slid behind the wheel, she climbed in the passenger side and reached for her seatbelt, saying, "So are you going to tell me what went on in there?"

He glanced back and took in the chief, who was looking out the window now, right at him. He started his Jeep, put it in gear, backed out, and said, "When I figure it out, I'll let you know."

❧

"YOU SURE YOU don't want something added to that coffee to warm you?" Mark said.

Billy Jo took in the view, the rocky shore below the small deck of the cabin where Mark Friessen lived. The dog he kept saying wasn't his was curled up beside him.

She sat in an old camping chair, her sunglasses on, with a mug of coffee, very aware of the bottle of whiskey on the ground beside Mark after he had taken a splash in his. He was complex, difficult. She realized now that he was the only one here who understood how she felt.

"Nope, the coffee's good," she said. "You still haven't told me what the chief said to you."

She thought of Shay, who'd been so excited that just maybe, she'd get to see her sister. She didn't think she'd ever forget the hate Shay had unleashed on her while being yanked out of there by the Feds.

"He told me to take a few days off, get my head straight, and be okay with not keeping my promise to Shay."

She could see he was still bothered. From the way he lifted his gaze and looked out to the ocean, she couldn't help wondering what he was thinking.

"But the thing is," he said, "I was raised better than that. My word is everything." He was wearing sunglasses, but now, as he looked at her, she realized there was more.

"So what does that mean? Shay's gone. The Feds have her."

"You know her father, the man I mentioned?"

Billy Jo nodded.

"I had already reached out to him and talked to him," he said.

Her head went, as it always did, to the mother who had tossed her away. Her lead, the only one she had, was her last known location in the San Juan Islands. "So you didn't lie about that."

He shook his head. "No. I did it when I was supposed to be putting the file away. No one was talking about who was hurting Shay. The man didn't know he had two daughters, twins. He had known their mother only briefly before shipping out overseas. He wants them in his life."

"So the whole thing with the bus ticket…"

An odd smile touched his lips. "To her father—who, by the way, should have contacted social services by now. I didn't lie, but I didn't tell her everything. So why did Shay not come clean about who hurt her?"

There was so much he didn't understand, she thought. "Trust. You should know that while we sat at your desk before the agents came in, she told me about that knife she pulled on her foster brother. She was defending herself. She'd been in the shower, and he popped the lock and walked right in. He'd done it before. She feared what he'd do, so she started carrying a small knife. She had it in the shower with her. She grabbed it as he ripped back the curtain. The foster parents never reported that part. The bruising on her back and legs was from her first night in juvie. Two girls held her down, and one of the guards stood and watched."

She wasn't sure she'd ever seen Mark so shocked. "You have no idea," she said, "just like everyone out there, what really goes on behind closed and locked doors. I lived with foster parents, lived through the abuse, and it was always put on me. I just learned early to shut myself off and swallow it and take it. I hope Shay's father shows up for her. Do you really think this thing was just Nora and Jeannette and a super fancy house rental?"

He shook his head and leaned forward, and she took in the ink from a tattoo that poked from beneath the sleeve of his T-shirt. "Nope," he said. "I guarantee you that's a great cover. There's not an owner around who wouldn't know something like that was going on in their house. Likely, the owner is a part of it. Seems this was the perfect crime, wrapped up nice and neat, and we were tossed the small fish in the pond. This goes way bigger than two women. I suspect this island is a stop along the way in an organization with a lot of arms— but then, as my chief put it, what do I know? I'm just a small-time detective, and this case has now been closed. The Feds are in charge, and the chief has some order restored on the island. What I still can't figure out, though, is the shooting and explosion at CJ's place yesterday. CJ wasn't even there when I went up. He was off the island for the day. Every local knows about CJ and his guns, his shenanigans. His doors are unlocked…"

"A great distraction."

He shrugged. "Sure, but why, if they ended up letting her go?"

"Let me guess: You like everything neat and tidy, and unsolved puzzles drive you crazy."

He didn't smile, and she found herself staring at his tattoo again, which looked like a face, before he replied, "I don't like mysteries that can't be solved. So what's next for you on this island, Billy Jo McCabe?"

What could she say? She had her own mystery to solve, that of the mother who'd left her in a system that had nearly killed her. The resentment she felt over that was something she'd never shared. "Oh, same old. By the way, what is that on your arm, a picture?"

He hesitated, then lifted his sleeve to reveal the image of a woman, pretty.

"Why do you have a tattoo of a woman on your arm?" she said.

For a moment, as he leaned back in his chair and glanced out to the ocean, she wondered whether he'd answer. Then he said, "As a reminder that only fools fall in love. I was nearly married once, then got my heart crushed three times. She's the last one to have had a go at me."

She realized, as she stared at him, that he was serious. "Okay, that's kind of permanent, don't you think? What happens when one day you meet Mrs. Right and do get married? How do you think she'll respond to the image of another woman tattooed on your arm?"

There was an edge to his smile. "Not this guy. I took an oath to stay single forever. What about you, Billy Jo? Do you have some mystery guy tucked away in a corner somewhere, some far reach of the country?"

She thought of the only two times she'd dated and the disasters they had been. "Nope," she said. "Seems maybe we have something in common."

"And that is?"

"Staying single. It's not as bad as people make it out to be. Why, I have a cat who keeps me company and a job that fills me with meaning."

And she had the search for the woman who had abandoned her, who was out there somewhere. Sometimes, a mystery that needed to be solved was the only company she needed.

"Right." He lifted his mug to her. "To being single and happy."

"And not having to answer to anyone," she added.

Turn the page for a sneak peek of
HIDING IN PLAIN SIGHT the next book in the *BILLY JO
MCCABE MYSTERY*
Available in print, eBook & audio

What's next in the Billy Jo
McCabe Mystery

A long-buried secret that was never meant to be uncovered could suddenly put a target on both Detective Mark Friessen and Billy Jo McCabe.

Twenty-five years ago, Billy Jo was born to a meth addict and spent her first few months being weaned off the drug. Labeled a difficult baby, she was bounced from foster home to foster home. Later, she was called trouble, a runner, and was accused of starting fires and stealing. She pulled a knife on one foster brother and threatened to bash in the head of another, then spent time in jail by the age of fifteen. That was before she pulled a gun at a gas station and was adopted by Chase McCabe. Her file was then sealed.

However, Billy Jo feels growing resentment for the woman responsible for her first fifteen years of hell, the one who tossed her away as if she were garbage. That has her seeking out leads as to where her real mother is, her last known whereabouts based on the sealed file she isn't technically supposed to access. But following the rules is not something Billy Jo is known for, especially not when she's playing amateur detective, asking about a woman who evidently doesn't want to be found.

Before long, Detective Mark Friessen shows up on her doorstep after someone files a complaint against her, warning her about harassing the locals. But then Billy Jo finds herself terrorized by someone determined to stop her from uncovering the truth.

Trusting anyone in her search could come at a cost, as Billy Jo soon learns that when her mother disappeared, she took with her a secret that someone doesn't want unearthed. Ultimately, her quest for answers puts a target on her that could see her killed, and that leaves Billy Jo once again forced to trust Mark, a man she will likely always be at odds with.

When Billy Jo thought of Carly Thornton, never in a million years had she pictured a white picket fence.

She parked on the street, looking out at the house, a cute two-story craftsman with teal trim and a front porch with two comfy lounge chairs, a welcoming invitation to come sit and visit. She took a second to check whether she had the right address.

This had to be a joke.

She couldn't pry her hands from where they were wrapped around her black steering wheel, the car still idling. She took in the houses on both sides of the street, the kind of homes that implied family, community, respectability, where people likely spent Saturdays barbecuing with neighbors.

This had to be the wrong Carly Thornton. But then, the trail had gone cold here after so much digging. The curiosity Billy Jo hadn't been able to shake suddenly turned into anger, which had her turning off the car, yanking on the door handle, and stepping out, unable to pull her eyes from the respectable neighborhood around her.

This was a mistake. Perhaps she had been wrong about the name. After all, Carly Thornton must have been a common name, like Jane Smith. She hesitated as soon as the thought hit her, though. After all her digging, following this cold trail, she knew that the last known location of her mother—scratch that, of the woman who'd given birth to her, was here. And how many people named Carly Jane Thornton, with the same birthdate, with a mother whose maiden name was Holloway, could be living on the island?

The records had huge gaps in time and a ton of inaccuracies, as if Carly didn't want to be found, but then, with a father like Chase McCabe, who could literally find a needle in a haystack, Billy Jo had learned from the best.

She gave her door a shove closed and left it parked on the narrow street, hearing the sounds of the morning, sprinklers running and a dog barking. She put one foot in front of the other and started walking up to the driveway. The grass was carefully manicured and green even though most of the island was facing a water shortage, and the perennials and bushes appeared well cared for.

She fisted her hands, feeling the curiosity that had driven her building in the pit of her stomach again. Wearing sandals and faded green capris, she looped her baggy purse over her shoulder and took in the car in the driveway, a silver BMW, only a few years old. Everything about the house appeared pristine, neat and tidy, nothing like what she'd expected from an addict.

The inside door was closed, and the screen door was

white. Her heartbeat kicked up as she tapped on it, and it rattled. She heard footsteps, feeling her rage building, a frown pulling at her lips. Her heart thumped once, long and loud, as the door opened, and she stared into blue eyes, dark hair, and a smile she hadn't expected.

"Hello. Can I help you?"

It was her voice, soft. She didn't appear that old, and she wasn't much taller than Billy Jo, about five foot two. She pushed open the screen, and Billy Jo glimpsed inside the house behind her, seeing gleaming hardwood and nice furnishings, hearing voices and footsteps from what she thought was the kitchen.

"I'm looking for Carly Thornton. My name is Billy Jo McCabe. I hope this doesn't sound totally strange, but the searches I've done show that this house is where she lives."

The woman's smile suddenly faltered, and she didn't know what to make of her expression.

"Are you Carly?" Billy Jo finally asked.

"You have the wrong house," the woman said. "I've never heard of Carly Thornton. Who are you, anyway —a bill collector, a solicitor? The sign clearly says we don't accept any here." She pointed to a sign by the door, *No soliciting*.

So she didn't like strange people showing up. Billy Jo knew well when someone was uncomfortable, though. She could tell from the tension in her expression.

"Carly, who's at the door?" a man called out.

Billy Jo heard his footsteps before he appeared behind the woman. About her dad's age, he had dark hair and hazel eyes, and he smiled, holding a mug of coffee. His hand rested on the woman's shoulder.

"Oh, just someone who's lost and looking for directions, is all," the woman said. "Can you see that the girls finish breakfast and get ready for school? We're running late already."

Billy Jo stood in silence, watching. The man was tall, solidly built, wearing blue jeans, a golf shirt, and a wedding ring. He looked over to her and back to the woman, and the two exchanged the kind of look a husband and wife shared. "Don't be long, then," he said. "You said you had to leave earlier for the school meeting, and don't forget we have the Davidson fundraiser tonight."

Then he stepped away from the door, and the woman angled her head to him and gave him a smile. As he walked away, though, and she dragged her gaze back to Billy Jo, her face was filled with the kind of unfriendliness she hadn't seen in a long time.

"So you are Carly?" Billy Jo said, the heaviness inside her now building into a sick feeling.

"Look, I don't know who you are or what you want, but I asked nicely," the woman said. "Please go away. I already told you that you have the wrong house." She actually stepped out and pulled the inside door closed quietly behind her, holding the screen so it wouldn't slap closed.

Secrets and lies. She knew when someone was holding out on her. Billy Jo had to step back, really taking in this woman, who was of the same height and build as her. Her hair reached her shoulders, and she was dressed casually, much like Billy Jo. The panic and something else in her expression said she didn't want Billy Jo asking about Carly Thornton.

"I don't know why you're pretending you're not her," Billy Jo said. "By your reaction, only a fool would miss that you're hiding something. Let me tell you that finding you wasn't easy. The trail was hidden and cold, and someone went to a lot of trouble to make it that way. I didn't have a clue what I was going to say to you, but here it is. I was born twenty-five years ago in a small Nevada town, on June 15th, to a meth addict. I spent my first few months being weaned off the drug. As a baby, I was difficult to care for, and I was in and out of the ER, being bounced around from foster home to foster home. I think, by your face, your expression, your reaction to me, that you're my mother. I've been looking for you for a really long time. But what I can't understand is this picture-perfect life you have now, or how you just abandoned me to the hell I lived through for fifteen years until I was finally adopted by my parents…"

"Look," the woman said. "This Carly Thornton you say you're looking for is not me. She doesn't exist. I'm sorry for what you've been through, and it sounds horrible, but that's not on me. I would appreciate you not coming back here again. Please leave. I wish you the best of luck finding this woman, but she's not me. Now, if you don't mind, I need to get back to my family and get my girls ready for school." She was still holding the door, and the expression on her face was guarded.

"I don't know what you're hiding or why you want to pretend this isn't you, but I think I deserve some answers," Billy Jo said. "I have a right. No, I demand—"

"You have no right to anything," the woman said, cutting her off quite sharply. She took a step toward her, letting the screen door close and forcing Billy Jo back closer to the steps. Her voice was low and quiet. "I'm going to ask you just one more time: Please leave, please. I have a good life here, a husband, children. You said you were adopted, you have a mother and father? Good, because they're your family. It sounds to me as if you're looking to dig up a problem that should stay buried. Don't bring this to my doorstep, trying to search for answers down memory lane. It's not going to happen." She reached for the screen door and pulled it open, then for the knob of the closed inside door.

"Wait, please," Billy Jo said. She could feel this slipping away, this opportunity to look the woman she hated in the eye, but this was nothing like what she'd expected. "I know you're her. I just want some answers, please."

"Carly Thornton no longer exists. I'm sorry for whatever happened to you, but by the looks of it, you appear to be doing fine. As you said, you have a family who adopted you. That was a long time ago. Please go away—and don't come back. Please." There was nothing friendly in her tone, and the way she looked at Billy Jo with such anger, hate, and fear tore open that giant wound inside her that had never really healed.

Billy Jo put her hands on the screen door before the woman could close it, but the woman still moved to open the inside door. "Look, I just want some questions answered. I'll come back another time so we can talk, but I think I deserve that much."

All the woman did was step back inside and shake her head, then said in a low voice, "Please go, please, and don't come back. You're entitled to nothing."

Then the door closed in her face.

Billy Jo looked over to the living room window as she turned to take a step down. Two girls, maybe eight and ten, had parted the blinds and were looking out before the woman pulled them away.

She stepped down the two steps from the porch,

taking in this perfection, the perfect life this woman now had. So that was Carly Thornton, who was nothing like the meth-addicted woman who'd abandoned her.

Instead of resolving anything, the meeting had left rage bubbling up inside her. Carly had dumped her and had been responsible for her childhood of hell, and now she got a free pass to have a great life?

As she walked back to her car, looking once more at the perfect house, the perfect yard, and the image of a perfect family, she felt like garbage, unwanted. She knew there was no way this woman was getting a pass.

No, she'd keep coming back, and she'd figure out a way to get the answers she wanted, the answers she deserved. There was no way she was going to let herself be a dirty little secret Carly was trying to forget. Billy Jo was going to make damned sure her birth mother told her everything.

About the Author

"Lorhainne Eckhart is one of my go to authors when I want a guaranteed good book. So many twists and turns, but also so much love and such a strong sense of family."

(Lora W., Reviewer)

New York Times & USA Today bestseller Lorhainne Eckhart is best known for her writing Raw Relatable Real Romances, where "Morals and family are running themes. Danger, romance, and a drive to do what is right will see you glued to the page." As one fan calls her, she is the "Queen of the family saga." (aherman) writing "the ups and downs of what goes on within a family but also with some suspense, angst and of course a bit of romance thrown in for good measure." Follow Lorhainne on Bookbub to receive alerts on New Releases and Sales and join her mailing list at LorhainneEckhart.com for her Monday Blog, books news, giveaways and FREE reads. With over 120 books, audiobooks, and multiple series published and available at all retailers now translated into six languages. She is a multiple recipient of the Readers' Favorite Award for Suspense and Romance, and lives in the Pacific Northwest on an island, is the mother of three, her oldest has autism and she is an advocate for never giving up on your dreams.

"Lorhainne Eckhart has this uncanny way of just hitting the spot every time with her books."

(Caroline L., Reviewer)

The O'Connells: *The O'Connells of Livingston, Montana are not your typical family. A riveting collection of stories surrounding the ups and downs of what goes on within a family but also with some suspense, angst and of course a bit of romance thrown in for good measure "I thought I loved the Friessens, but I absolutely adore the O'Connell's. Each and every book has totally different genres of stories but the one thing in common is how she is able to wrap it around the family which is the heart of each story." (C. Logue)*

The Friessens: *An emotional big family romance series, the Friessen family siblings find their relationships tested, lay their hearts on the line, and discover lasting love! "Lorhainne Eckhart is one of my go to authors when I want a guaranteed good book. So many twists and turns, but also so much love and such a strong sense of family." (Lora W., Reviewer)*

__The Parker Sisters:__ The Parker Sisters are a close-knit family, and like any other family they have their ups and downs. "Eckhart has crafted another intense family drama… The character development is outstanding, and the emotional investment is high…" (Aherman, Reviewer)

__The McCabe Brothers:__ Join the five McCabe siblings on their journeys to the dark and dangerous side of love! An intense, exhilarating collection of romantic thrillers you won't want to miss. — "Eckhart has a new series that is definitely worth the read. The queen of the family saga started this series with a spin-off of her wildly successful Friessen series." From a Readers' Favorite award—winning author and "queen of the family saga" (Aherman)

__Billy Jo McCabe Mystery:__ The social worker and the cop, an unlikely couple drawn together on a small, secluded Pacific Northwest island where nothing is as it seems. Protecting the innocent comes at a cost, and what seems to be a sleepy, quiet town is anything but.

Lorhainne loves to hear from her readers! You can connect with me at:
www.LorhainneEckhart.com
lorhainneeckhart.le@gmail.com

 facebook.com/AuthorLorhainneEckhart

twitter.com/LEckhart

instagram.com/lorhainneeckhart

bookbub.com/profile/lorhainne-eckhart

pinterest.com/lorhainneeckhart

Also by Lorhainne Eckhart

The Outsider Series
The Forgotten Child (Brad and Emily)
A Baby and a Wedding *(An Outsider Series Short)*
Fallen Hero (Andy, Jed, and Diana)
The Search *(An Outsider Series Short)*
The Awakening (Andy and Laura)
Secrets (Jed and Diana)
Runaway (Andy and Laura)
Overdue *(An Outsider Series Short)*
The Unexpected Storm (Neil and Candy)
The Wedding (Neil and Candy)

The Friessens: A New Beginning
The Deadline (Andy and Laura)
The Price to Love (Neil and Candy)
A Different Kind of Love (Brad and Emily)
A Vow of Love, A Friessen Family Christmas

The Friessens
The Reunion
The Bloodline (Andy & Laura)
The Promise (Diana & Jed)
The Business Plan (Neil & Candy)
The Decision (Brad & Emily)
First Love (Katy)
Family First
Leave the Light On
In the Moment

In the Family
In the Silence
In the Charm
Unexpected Consequences
It Was Always You
The First Time I Saw You
Welcome to My Arms
Welcome to Boston
I'll Always Love You
Ground Rules
A Reason to Breathe
You Are My Everything
Anything For You
The Homecoming
Stay Away From My Daughter
The Bad Boy
A Place of Our Own
The Visitor
All About Devon
Long Past Dawn
How to Heal a Heart
Keep Me In Your Heart

The O'Connells

The Neighbor
The Third Call
The Secret Husband
The Quiet Day
The Commitment
The Missing Father
The Hometown Hero
Justice
The Family Secret

The Fallen O'Connell
The Return of the O'Connells
And The She Was Gone
The Stalker
The O'Connell Family Christmas
The Girl Next Door

The McCabe Brothers
Don't Stop Me (Vic)
Don't Catch Me (Chase)
Don't Run From Me (Aaron)
Don't Hide From Me (Luc)
Don't Leave Me (Claudia)
Out of Time

A Billy Jo McCabe Mystery
Nothing As it Seems
Hiding in Plain Sight
The Cold Case
The Trap
Above the Law

The Wilde Brothers
The One (Joe and Margaret)
The Honeymoon, A Wilde Brothers Short
Friendly Fire (Logan and Julia)
Not Quite Married, A Wilde Brothers Short
A Matter of Trust (Ben and Carrie)
The Reckoning, A Wilde Brothers Christmas
Traded (Jake)
Unforgiven (Samuel)
The Holiday Bride

Married in Montana
His Promise
Love's Promise
A Promise of Forever

The Parker Sisters
Thrill of the Chase
The Dating Game
Play Hard to Get
What We Can't Have
Go Your Own Way
A June Wedding

Kate & Walker
One Night
Edge of Night
Last Night

Walk the Right Road Series
The Choice
Lost and Found
Merkaba
Bounty
Blown Away: The Final Chapter

The Saved Series
Saved
Vanished
Captured

Single Titles
He Came Back
Loving Christine

For my German Readers
Die Außenseiter-Reihe
Der Vergessene Junge
Der Gefallene Held

For my French Readers
L'ENFANT OUBLIÉ

www.ingramcontent.com/pod-product-compliance
Lightning Source LLC
Chambersburg PA
CBHW032013180726

48283CB00008B/2656